A GRATEFUL
HARVEST

PRAIRIE RIVER

A GRATEFUL
HARVEST

KRISTIANA GREGORY

SCHOLASTIC INC.
New York Toronto London Auckland Sydney
Mexico   os Aires

ISBN 0-439-43993-0

12 11 10 9 8 7 6 5 4 3 2   3 4 5 6 7 8/0
                                                                    40

Printed in the U.S.A.
First printing, November 2003

Table of Contents

1 - Along the River 1

2 - A Warning 7

3 - Nessa's Trunk 13

4 - The Rescue 17

5 - Fanny Jo's Secret 22

6 - A Terrible Mistake 28

7 - Broken Fence 34

8 - A Fine Leather Shoe 39

9 - The Blacksmith 44

10 - School Begins 49

11 - A Curious Visitor 53

12 - Harvest 59

13 - Letter 65

14 - A Dirt Patch 70

15 - Loaves and Fish 74

16 - Ivy 81

17 - A Friend Loves at All Times 87

18 - Fog 91

19 - Saturday Supper 98

20 - A Sack of Carrots 102

21 - The Thief 105

22 - The Old Mountain Man 111

23 - An Anonymous Donor 115

24 - A Perfect Fit 120

25 - Good News 124

26 - A Cloud in the Distance 127

27 - Green 133

28 - Under the Blanket 137

29 - "They're All Here" 140

30 - No Job 143

31 - A Small Idea 149

32 - He Answers 152

33 - Something New 156

34 - The Library 161

35 - All in One Day.. 167

36 - A Debt Paid 173

37 - Invitation 177

38 - Abraham Lincoln Said 180

39 - One Gray Afternoon..................................... 186

40 - Where the Wind Always Blows.................... 190

PRAIRIE RIVER

A GRATEFUL HARVEST

CHAPTER ONE

―◆◆―

Along the River

The prairie spread as far as Nessa could see, pale yellow under the hot August sun. She sat beside Peter's grave listening to the wind hiss through the tall grass. The tree her students had planted in his memory was too little to offer much shade, but its leaves rustled with promise. She could hardly believe it had been just a few weeks ago. Nessa pressed her fingers into the soil around the tree's trunk. She smiled at the dampness. One of the children must have come already from the creek with a pail.

"Miss Vanessa," they told her after his funeral, "someday it's gonna be the prettiest, proudest tree in Prairie River. You'll see."

And she was certain that not a day had passed without one of them watering it, sometimes twice or even three times in an afternoon. In such heat, this young oak tree would need as much water as possible to help its roots grow deep.

Often Nessa visited the cemetery with her puppy. Though the pup's name was Green, she was the color of a lion cub, tawny, with a soft mane. She had the floppy ears of a water dog and big paws. Already she'd proven to be a good swimmer and was now drying off from playing in the river. It was peaceful here, just the two of them. When Nessa felt clammed up with worries, she could come here to rest and think.

Such as now. At this moment, the school committee was voting on whether Nessa should be rehired as the teacher. Knowing people were talking about her made her nervous. And she felt heartsick to think the children might no longer be her students.

Nessa raised the hem of her gingham dress above her knees to cool off, and untied her shoes. They had fit fine when she ran away from the orphanage, but that was nearly five months ago. Now they were tight and hurt her feet. She wanted to cool down. With abandon, she kicked them off, then rolled down her stockings and flung them into the air. The wind caught them like leaves, floating them onto a nearby gravestone. Next, she pulled the ribbons from her braids and shook them loose. Her hair blew free. It felt wonderful.

While Green occupied herself by pawing at a rabbit hole, Nessa looked toward town. It was actually Fort Larned, one of the few signs of civilization in central Kansas. A flagpole stood one hundred feet above the parade ground, surrounded by soldiers' barracks and other sod buildings.

From the knoll where she sat, Nessa had a sweeping view of the Santa Fe Trail and the freight wagons approaching the fort. Despite the distance, she could hear the rattling of harnesses from teams of oxen and shouts from their drivers. Dust rose from the trail only to be whisked sideways by the wind. The year was 1865. Troops were here to help keep peace with several tribes of Indians and to protect travelers.

Pawnee Creek glistened in the sunlight. It flowed along two sides of the fort then east toward the schoolhouse. From this distance Nessa could see the school's roof, but its sod walls were hidden behind a swell of land. She wished she could see the horses and wagons that waited out front, but maybe it was better this way. She thought of the committee members who were inside discussing her qualifications. Some of them didn't like her and others simply wanted her to return to Independence, Missouri, her former home.

Since Peter's death last month, many of the townsfolk criticized Nessa for letting him out of her sight during the Fourth of July picnic. *How could a teacher be so careless with one of her own students?* They whispered this among themselves, just loud enough for her to hear.

With a heavy sigh, Nessa lay back in the grass. She liked that no one could see her here. Sometimes it felt good to be invisible. The memory of that terrible Independence Day wouldn't go away. Nessa still played the wretched events over in her mind, but she took comfort in two things: First, Peter's father, Lieutenant Sullivan, and his mother, Mrs. Sullivan, didn't blame her. They knew how Nessa adored their son and how he had adored her. They even gave her one of Peter's puppies from Yellow Dog. Now every time Nessa petted Green, it helped her remember that she'd been forgiven.

The second thing that comforted Nessa was knowing Peter was in heaven with Jesus, where there were no more tears or sorrow. She believed she would see him again one day, as she would her own mother and father.

Nessa felt safe lying there, watching the wide blue sky, which today was crowned with clouds rolling and changing shape in the wind. Spreading her arms, she could feel the prickle of dried brush through her sleeves. When her puppy flopped next to her and fell into an instant sleep, Nessa closed her eyes, too. The aroma of sun-drenched soil made her feel drowsy. Sometimes it seemed she could sleep forever.

A sudden chittering of meadowlarks woke her. The birds flushed up from the flowers as if startled. Nessa bolted upright, slipping her fingers under Green's collar to pull her close.

Something was moving through the towering grass. Her heart froze, remembering the rattlesnake that had bitten Peter. If a six-year-old couldn't survive its poison, she probably wouldn't, either. She held Green tight, realizing with horror that whatever was approaching was much larger than a snake.

Oh, Jesus, she prayed silently, *whatever is coming this way, please . . .*

A hum of mosquitoes rose from the grass as it parted like a curtain. An Indian boy appeared, his braids hanging over his bare chest. A breechcloth made from an animal skin had tufts of black and white fur that moved in the wind. The sharp odor of skunk made her eyes sting.

Nessa drew in a breath, afraid to move. She felt faint from the heat and her mouth went dry. She guessed he was near her age, fourteen perhaps. His knees were muddy, and a cut along his shin had a black scab. His moccasins were adorned with blue beads around each ankle.

They stared at each other. Nessa's mind raced. How could she forget that warriors had killed two sutlers earlier this summer? Could this boy be from the same tribe? Was he going to hurt her?

Green was wagging her tail, but Nessa held on to her collar to keep her from playing with the stranger. Now she wished she hadn't taken off her shoes. If she carried her dog and started running, she might be able to get away but she wasn't used to going barefoot. There were briars and coarse grasses that could cut her feet. And if the Indian grabbed her no one would hear her scream. He continued to stare at her.

Nessa felt her heart pounding beneath her blouse. She tried to make herself breathe slowly and as she did, a thought occurred to her: *Maybe this boy is just curious.* She remembered the terrifying afternoon when she and Minnie had been in the schoolhouse this summer, when some Indians approached on horseback and rode in circles around the building. Finally, the riders had left without causing any harm. She remembered what she had said to reassure Minnie then.

They were just curious, and we don't need to hate them for that. Nessa now found comfort in those words.

Still, she wasn't sure what to do. In case she needed to run from him, she stood up. Brushing off her skirt, she glanced his way. She noticed his horse waiting nearby. Its tail swished at the flies on its flank. There was no saddle. Its mane was braided with beads and a large white feather hung from its forelock. Nessa had never seen such a beautiful animal; it was the color of chocolate. She wished she could pet it.

A moment passed. The boy's face showed no emotion, but his eyes seemed warm. They were dark brown.

With her heart in her throat, Nessa offered a greeting. "Uh . . . hello."

At the sound of her voice, he turned away and with a swift leap landed on the back of his horse. Breaking into a gallop, he headed for the bottomlands and then disappeared along the river.

CHAPTER TWO

A Warning

When Nessa ran up the steps to the boardinghouse, Mrs. Lockett was there sweeping the porch. She was a stout woman with blond hair piled atop her head.

"Mercy, child," she said, "how come your shoes ain't on? Just look at your poor feet."

"An Indian . . ." Nessa was out of breath.

"Sit here, honey, while you catch your wherewithal and tell me what happened. Minnie," she called through the open door, "fetch us some water, will you, darlin'?"

Nessa's hair was auburn and hung down her back in windblown curls. In her hurry to reach town she had grabbed her shoes and stockings, but hadn't taken time to put them on. Even after she realized she wasn't being chased, she didn't know why she couldn't slow herself down to put them on. Now her feet were bleeding from thorns. Her cheeks were flushed.

Mrs. Lockett took off her apron and began cleaning Nessa's cuts with it. The woman, who ran a boarding-house out of her home, had been like a mother to Nessa since her arrival in Prairie River four months ago. "And so, my dear, what did you see? Thank you, Minnie, set the pail there."

Mrs. Lockett's daughter, six years old with blond pigtails, filled a dipper with water and handed it to Nessa, who was still breathing hard. They smiled at each other, and Nessa recounted the details of what had just happened.

"Maybe he was Cheyenne," said Nessa after she related her story. "But I don't know. How can you tell the tribes apart?"

"Well," said Mrs. Lockett, "I suspect the interpreters here at the fort know who's who. This boy could've been a Cheyenne, but there're also Arapaho, Kiowa, and Comanches around here. I just thank God you're back safe and sound, honey. We'll need to let the fort commander know what you saw but that no harm was done. Meanwhile, Mr. Applewood was here lookin' for you, Nessa. The committee finished its votin'. You best head over to the store."

Two sutlers' stores were located outside the perimeter of the fort. Here soldiers could buy chewing tobacco, cocoa, whiskey, canned oysters, and other items not furnished by the army. They even sold hoopskirts for soldiers' wives, and washboards and clothespins for the army's laundresses. The townspeople relied on these stores as well.

Mr. Applewood, who was the head of the school committee, owned one of these stores. It was built of stone and was in a compound with their sod house, a corral, workshop, and billiard hall where soldiers entertained themselves in the evenings.

The path from the boardinghouse where Nessa lived with the Locketts followed Pawnee Creek toward town. On her way, she hummed a song she heard in church last Sunday. Though she didn't remember the words, it made her feel better. She dreaded facing Mr. Applewood and his wife.

"There, there," Mrs. Lockett had said as she helped Nessa freshen up. She brushed the snarls from Nessa's hair then wove it into one thick braid. "Honey, just be yourself and never mind how they treat you."

Along the path, Nessa looked down at her scuffed shoes and wished they didn't squeeze her feet, which hurt even more since her run home. The wind blew her dress against her legs, revealing her petticoat. She also wished her skirt was longer, at least to cover her ankles. It embarrassed her to be growing out of her clothes and that the worn spots at her elbows were patched.

Shading her eyes from the hot sun, Nessa looked up to see a soldier riding along the trail. He carried an American flag and was part of the cavalry unit escorting a stagecoach to the fort. Usually the sight of the stage thrilled Nessa because it could mean a letter for her. But not today. She was still uneasy from her encounter with the Indian boy, and she felt nervous about what the committee may have decided.

How she wanted to be a teacher! She had come to love the children. She had so enjoyed instructing them last term and felt she had learned from them as well. The salary of nine dollars a month seemed a fortune to Nessa and she was grateful for it. Though she did chores for Mrs. Lockett to earn her keep, she still needed spending money.

And there was a debt she was trying to pay off. At the orphanage, her beloved teacher, Miss Eva, had loaned her twenty dollars to help start her new life. Nessa wanted to repay her. Without that loan, she would never have escaped to Prairie River.

Above all, Nessa wanted to prove to herself that she could make it on her own. If she failed, she told herself she would have to return to Missouri.

The grim thought of what awaited her there made her stomach feel swirly. The orphanage headmaster had given her only two options. Either she must become a servant or she had to marry the bland Reverend McDuff. Nessa shivered at the thought that Reverend McDuff believed Nessa was ordained to be his wife. He said the Lord had told him so.

But the Lord didn't tell me, Nessa reminded herself as she headed to the store. *Besides, I don't love him,* she thought. Once again, she was glad she had run away before the marriage ceremony.

A bell jingled when Nessa opened the door. It was cool inside the stone building. Mrs. Applewood was behind the counter weighing a ham. Her hair was combed up into a tight bun, and the collar of her dress was buttoned to her chin. When she saw Nessa, she shook her head.

"He's been waiting for you an hour now," she said, "but guess you don't respect others who work for a living, do you?"

"Hello, Mrs. Applewood." Nessa was careful not to say Apple*worm*, which is what she thought every time she saw the woman's sour face. Nessa had accidentally called her by that name three times. *Mrs. Appleworm.* And three times, she had forced herself to mumble an apology.

Nessa carried several coins in her pocket. She put a penny on the counter. "A stick of peppermint, please," she said. "I'm sorry you've had to wait." Nessa tried to hide her hurt feelings. It upset her to be scolded every time she came into this place.

"Tom," the woman called to her husband in a back room. "The girl's here, finally decided to show up." Mrs. Applewood uncorked one of the large jars of candy, took out a striped peppermint, and broke it in half. She handed the smaller piece to Nessa, then took her penny.

"It's about time," said the man coming out from behind a curtain. He wore an apron over his blue shirt and his beard was neatly trimmed. A pair of spectacles sat on his nose.

"Vanessa Ann Clemens." He looked at Nessa's shoulder as he spoke. "You might as well hear the truth. The committee voted to find another teacher, someone more suitable to protecting the children and who would set a good example with regard to manners and showing respect. We spent all morning trying to figure out who that might be. As you know, schoolteachers aren't allowed to be married, but the only ones at the fort who are *not* married are some of the laundresses and a servant or two. We doubt any of them even know how to read. Then there's you. A fourteen-year-old orphan whom nobody knows much about. We realize that until someone better comes along, we're stuck with you."

Though his words were unkind, Nessa felt her heart quicken. "Do you mean, oh, Mr. Applewood, are you saying I've been rehired?"

"Yes, girl, I'm afraid so. There's one other thing, however."

"Yes, sir?" The peppermint suddenly felt sticky in her hand. She couldn't wait to hurry home to tell Mrs. Lockett the good news.

Mr. Applewood regarded Nessa over the tops of his eyeglasses. He pointed at her. "If anything happens to any of the children like last time, if there's even a breath of complaint, we will run you out of town so fast you won't have time to pack. Is that clear?"

Nessa couldn't answer because of the lump in her throat. Suddenly, her happy news didn't sound so happy after all. His harshness stung her. His words made her feel small and useless.

"I asked you, girl, is that clear?"

Too discouraged to speak, Nessa nodded and gave a quick curtsy, then turned for the door. She was not going to let the Applewoods see her cry.

CHAPTER THREE

Nessa's Trunk

Nessa rushed back to the boardinghouse. Too upset to speak, she went upstairs to her room where she often found solace. It was a cheerful place under a low, sloping roof. One window faced the morning sunlight with a view of the wide, golden prairie. The other looked out toward Fort Larned. Her room was so small that when sitting on her bed she could touch each wall by leaning a little to the left, then a little to the right. Her nightgown and apron hung from pegs behind the door.

A bowl with a pitcher of water sat on a bureau. There was no chamber pot like at the orphanage, but instead Nessa used the privy out back, as did everyone at Mrs. Lockett's boardinghouse.

The only other piece of furniture was Nessa's trunk. It was wedged under her window with just enough space for her knees so she could sit on her bed and use it as a writing table. It was two feet tall and made of tin, painted red and green. Oak ribs separated the two colors. The lid had silver corners and a silver latch.

This chest was new to Nessa, having been delivered to

Prairie River just a few weeks earlier. Miss Eva had found it in the attic of the orphanage and knew only by a tag on its lock that it belonged to Nessa. Ten years ago, a stranger had brought Nessa to the headmaster, Mr. Carey. She was just four and had no memory of that night or of having any luggage. Over the years, Mr. Carey never mentioned it to anyone so it had remained in the attic undisturbed.

The discovery of the trunk had been a revelation. When Nessa was finally able to look inside, she began uncovering remnants of the family she'd lost and forgotten. Though most of the items were a mystery to her, some discoveries brought great joy. Such as her father's Bible. From the family tree on the front pages she learned her middle name was Ann and that she was born in Racine, Wisconsin, ". . . at sunrise, on a cold spring morning, 1851." Her parents were Claire Christine and Howard Lewis Clemens. These clues about her past brought Nessa a peace that had long eluded her.

Still, there were unanswered questions. Many. Nessa's mother had died giving birth to twins. But the Bible listed only the date of *her* death, not of the babies'. Were they alive? And if so, where were they?

She examined a packet of letters bundled with blue ribbons. The first time Nessa had read them she felt embarrassed, as if she were peeking through a window into someone's parlor. It was like eavesdropping on her mother's private conversations.

Dear sister,
    The cottage is ready for summer visitors so I

do hope you and Howard will come soon with little Nessa. I miss my niece and remember fondly our upset in the canoe last summer. . . . Do come see me.

Your loving,

Britta

After again reading this dated letter from her aunt, Nessa dipped her quill in the ink pot, then tapped it against the rim so her pen wouldn't drip. Her stationery was a brown piece of paper given to her by the editor of the *Prairie River Journal.* He was kind and generous. After every edition, Mr. Button saved leftover newsprint for her and her students. The editor was one of her first friends, for they had sat together in a stagecoach on their long journey west.

Dear Aunt Britta, Nessa now wrote. She set her pen down, gazing out at the prairie and the pale clouds. It was hard to write to someone she didn't know. The heat was stifling upstairs and the breeze coming in through her open windows gave no relief.

What should I say? she wondered. Should she describe her days at the orphanage, then ask about the twins? They would be ten years old by now. The more Nessa thought, the more questions she wanted to ask, but did not know where to start. And she did not want to sound desperate with loneliness, though that's often how she felt. Would it be all right to ask how her father was killed? Or why Nessa was brought to Missouri all the way from Wisconsin?

As she stared out the window, she noticed a dark stain on the horizon. It was moving, as if a shadow of clouds. By now she had learned the shadow was actually a herd of grazing buffalo. The animals often came near the fort, lumbering along the banks of Pawnee Creek for water. Soldiers sometimes spent their off-duty time hunting them for their hides. And buffalo tongue was a delicacy at this isolated post. She remembered seeing some at the Applewoods' store earlier.

Nessa's eyes returned to her letter. She dipped her pen again.

Dear Aunt Britta,
WHERE ARE THE TWINS?!! Why didn't you come looking for me after Papa died?!! Why did you let them send me to an orphanage? Why are the Applewoods mean to me? And why . . .

Nessa crumpled her letter and threw it against the wall. She didn't know how to be pleasant about all the questions squeezing her thoughts. She flung herself on her bed, pulling Green to her for comfort. The puppy's soft fur smelled good from the sun.

"You're my best friend," she said through tears. Nessa felt even more lonely knowing she might have family who didn't know where she was.

CHAPTER FOUR

————◆————

The Rescue

A soft knock at Nessa's door distracted her. She dried her cheeks with her hem, embarrassed that she'd been feeling sorry for herself.

"Come in," she said.

Minnie stood in the doorway next to her brother, Rolly. He was fourteen and had her same blue eyes and straw-blond hair that always looked as if he needed a comb. His slingshot rested inside his suspender.

"Pardon us for interrupting," said Minnie, "but remember the little colt? The one in the army corral? It's lame and . . ."

". . . they're gonna shoot it," said Rolly.

"What? When?" Nessa remembered seeing the foal, knock-kneed and just old enough to be without its mother. "Oh, Rolly, we have to stop them."

She was on her feet, hurrying downstairs, Rolly and Minnie behind her. In the kitchen they rushed past Mrs. Lockett at the stove. She was pulling out a pan of bread pudding from the oven. Her face was red from the heat. Strands of damp hair curled at her neck.

"We'll be back soon," Nessa called, "to help you with supper."

Before Mrs. Lockett could respond, they were out the back door.

There were several corrals in Prairie River, the largest one attached to the army's livery stable. Here oxen and horses rested from their journeys along the Santa Fe Trail. The colt was standing in the shade of a sod barn. He was gray with black speckles.

They stood on the rungs of the fence and leaned in, whistling for it to come closer. It wore a rope halter.

"Easy, boy," said Nessa, reaching to pet him. The end of his nose felt like velvet and was cool to the touch. When she stroked his withers, he tossed his head, watching her with his gray eye.

"Don't worry," said Rolly. "I've been observin' him these past days. He's used to folks, but he's frisky."

Nessa kneeled to look through the fence at the colt's legs. "Where's he lame?"

"You can't see it except when he walks. His front hoof is overgrown and it turns in a bit. They say he'll never run far or fast, that's why he's no good for the cavalry or to pull a stagecoach. The corporal told me this morning he's no good a-tall. Then he said they'd shoot him this afternoon."

At that moment, a soldier walked into the corral with a curl of rope. His blue coat had brass buttons that shone in the sunlight. From his belt hung a holster that creaked as he moved. A small sack of cartridges rattled against the gun. His pants were tucked into knee-high boots, polished black. The brim of his cap shaded his face.

"What're you kids doing here?" he said. "It's no place to play, you'll scare the stock, now go on, git." He waved his arm to shoo them away. Then he tied the rope to the colt's halter and began leading it to the gate.

Nessa looked at Rolly in desperation. "Where's he going?" she asked.

Without waiting for an answer, she ran alongside the fence and called to the soldier, "Are you going to shoot him, mister?"

"It's Corporal to you, girl, and yes, you're exactly right. Now, like I told you, skedaddle."

Nessa glanced back at Rolly, unsure of what to do. When the soldier came out onto the path, she rushed forward. The little horse stood as high as her elbow and dragged its hoof slightly as it walked. Ignoring the man's shout to go away, she threw her arms around the colt's neck and hugged it as if it were her own.

"Please don't shoot him," she begged. "I'll take care of him. Please . . ."

"You're just a young'un. I've seen you around, no folks looking after you. It takes money to feed a horse — hay, oats, a safe place so wolves don't get it. There're wolves here, missy, in case you haven't noticed, and horse thieves, namely the Indians."

"We have a corral. . . . Don't we, Rolly?" Suddenly remembering she'd been rehired as the schoolteacher, she said, "And I have a job, nine dollars a month."

The man laughed. "Ain't you special? Why, laundresses here make forty a month for all their dirty work. You must not be worth much being hired for so cheap."

Nessa ignored his insult. "I'll take him off your hands right now, sir, and you won't have to waste a bullet. Won't have to haul away the body, either. Here, I'll pay you for him." Nessa took the remaining coins from her pocket and counted out fifty cents.

The corporal stopped. He squinted skyward as if pleading with God. For a long moment he was silent. Finally, he took the coins and dropped the rope at Nessa's feet.

"Got yourself a colt, missy," he said. "And if either of you ever bother me again I'll report you to the general. Now, like I said, git."

Nessa and Rolly led the colt home, taking a slow pace because of its limp. As Minnie ran ahead to announce the news to her mother, Nessa remembered something.

"Oh, no," she said to Rolly. "We didn't even ask your ma if she minds me taking on a horse. I hope she's not upset with me."

Rolly shrugged. "A young horse ain't half as bad as some of the travelers she puts up."

Mrs. Lockett was waiting for them in the yard. She held open the gate to their corral where two mules, a cow, and a horse watched the procession with curiosity. With her hands on her wide hips, she said, "The other day when I heard the cavalry had a lame foal, I figured you'd be the one to rescue it, Nessa. Now let's put him under the lean-to there for shade — he's too young to be standing in such heat. Mercy, it's hot as the kitchen out here."

"I'm so sorry we didn't ask you first, Mrs. Lockett, but the soldier was going to shoot him right away. . . . There wasn't time. . . . He seemed so alone. . . . I . . ." Nessa couldn't find the words to say what she really meant. She wanted to give the colt a chance, as Mrs. Lockett had done for her.

"There, there, Nessa, you did the right thing. But now you and Rolly're responsible. It'll need your care every single day. Got any idea what you'll call 'im?"

Nessa was running her fingers through the colt's tangled mane. "I like the name Wildwing." She looked to Rolly for approval. When his blue eyes lit up with a smile, Nessa said, "Yes, that's it. Wildwing."

"What a fine name," said Mrs. Lockett.

CHAPTER FIVE

Fanny Jo's Secret

The kitchen was hot and humid from a stew simmering. Mrs. Lockett kept one of the woodstove lids open so smoke from the fire would keep mosquitoes away. While Nessa helped prepare supper, Minnie put forks and spoons on the table for eight people. Rolly brought in a pail of water to heat for dishwashing.

Four gentlemen guests waited on the front porch for their supper. Two of them were playing backgammon, the board resting on their knees. The others were each reading a *Harper's Magazine* from the stack kept in the parlor. Though it was also hot outside, the porch was shaded and a light breeze moved the air. Nessa wished they could eat in the yard, but flies and yellow jackets would swarm over their food.

"Nessa dear, supper's still an hour away," said Mrs. Lockett. "I told the sisters we'd bring over their supper tonight, so would you mind taking this to them?" She handed Nessa a basket. Inside were meat sandwiches, a bowl of green beans, and an apple tart. A can of strawberries was on the bottom. She covered the food with a red cloth. "Fanny Jo's feeling poorly and could use some encouragement. The strawberries are a special treat, tell her. I do believe those girls are homesick."

Nessa carried the basket over her arm as she walked along the creek to the fort, Green trotting beside her. At Officers' Row, she stepped up onto the wooden sidewalk with a sense of purpose.

"Officers' daughters only," a woman yelled to her. "You know better than to be up here, and that goes for your dog, too."

"Afternoon, ma'am," Nessa called, waving cheerfully. She admired the woman's beautiful hoopskirt and her thin waist shaped by a corset. A baby carriage was at her side, in the shade of a parasol.

Despite the woman's order, Nessa continued on her way with no intention of stepping down from the sidewalk onto the dirt path. She liked the sound her shoes made on the planks. The walkway was the length of one block and reminded her of being in a real town with real stores. Nearly every time Nessa came this way someone would tell her to go away. But today the rebuke didn't upset her. She was the schoolteacher and on a mission.

Fort Larned was surrounded on two sides by Pawnee Creek. Its third side was protected by the broad, dried-up streambed of Prairie River, which was the landmark that gave the town its name. Along these banks were tents and sod buildings for the laundresses. It was called Suds Row, and it was Nessa's destination. Clotheslines were stretched between poles, and there were campfires with cauldrons of steaming water.

Even though Fanny Jo and Laura worked for the baker and were not laundresses, they were allowed to live here in a log hut. The sisters were new to Prairie River, too. They were from Pennsylvania and had come west on the same stagecoach as Nessa and the newspaperman, Mr. Button. Their plan had been to surprise Fanny Jo's husband. He was a lieutenant, and the sisters had planned to live on Officers' Row. But upon their arrival, they learned that just a week earlier he had been transferred to Fort Dodge — a two-day journey south. For reasons Fanny Jo never explained, her husband had instructed her to return immediately to Pennsylvania. Nessa knew it was a disappointment that had upset her greatly after coming such a far way. Even Nessa had been troubled by the news. She had ached for the sisters, remembering well what it felt like to be abandoned.

But instead of going back East, Fanny Jo and Laura decided to stay at Fort Larned and find a way to support themselves. Nessa was pleased they had chosen to make Prairie River their home.

Nessa knocked on their door. Her puppy curled up in the grass on the shady side of the building to wait.

"Why, hello there, Nessa," said Laura. "Mrs. Lockett said you'd be by. Do come in, please."

A square window with four panes let in sunlight, revealing two beds, a small wood-burning stove, and a table. Fanny Jo sat in a chair, her feet in a pan of cool water. She wore only her chemise. Her face was red, and she was fanning herself with a folded newspaper. Her hair, which was usually swept up on her head with combs, was in one long braid over her shoulder. She looked younger than her twenty years.

"Dear, it's so nice to see you," she said. "Excuse my scanty attire, but the heat has rendered me useless. How are you?"

"Everything's fine, thank you." Nessa described her earlier adventure, rescuing the colt. "All my life I've wanted a horse. I can hardly believe he's mine. Rolly said it'll be a good while before we'll be able to ride him — if ever — but I'm more than willing to wait. Oh, forgive my manners, Fanny Jo. I'm sorry you're not feeling well. May I set the table for you?"

"That would be lovely. I do hope you can stay for a while and visit with us. I'm delighted you have your own horse now. Just think how independent you'll be once he's full grown."

Nessa removed the cloth from her basket and began setting out the food. At the sight of canned strawberries, Laura clapped her hands with pleasure. She was a year younger than her sister.

"I do declare! Your Mrs. Lockett is a jewel." With a knife Laura carved into the can's lid, in the shape of an *X*, then carefully peeled back each corner with a thick cloth so she wouldn't cut her fingers. She poured the strawberries into a bowl and offered them to her sister. "Fanny Jo, these will be good for your condition."

Nessa looked up. "Condition? It's not serious, I hope."

Fanny Jo laughed. "Can you keep a secret, Nessa?"

"Of course . . . yes." Nessa loved intrigue. Since they met on the stagecoach, she had learned the sisters were from high society and their ancestors came to America aboard the *Mayflower*. Their father was a senator who also had served in President Lincoln's cabinet. But there was a shadow of mystery surrounding them that Nessa couldn't quite figure out. For one thing, she didn't know why the lieutenant had sent Fanny Jo away after she'd come such a long way to see him. And another thing Nessa didn't understand was why the sisters wanted to live in the middle of nowhere when they had wealthy parents back East who cared about them.

If only they knew what it was like to not have a mother or father, to not have anyone. But despite how different Nessa's background was from theirs, she liked the sisters and yearned to be their friend.

"All right," Nessa said. "I'm listening."

Laura spoke for her. "Fanny Jo's going to have a baby . . . at Christmastime!"

Nessa's eyes grew wide. "A baby?" She caught her breath remembering a conversation she'd overheard at the seamstress's shop. It seemed the ladies had believed Fanny Jo had a secret that would shame her family. Nessa hadn't heard everything they were saying, but the seamstress had made the situation sound serious indeed.

"Oh, my," said Nessa. She hesitated, wondering how to ask the next question. "That seems like wonderful news. Your husband must be happy, too?" Suddenly, Nessa wished she hadn't mentioned the lieutenant.

Fanny Jo shifted in her chair, dipping her wrists in the water to cool herself. "Well, you see," she said, "I haven't told him yet. And he doesn't know where we are. When we saw him at Fort Dodge in the beginning of May, he was so worried about our safety he sent me away, and he thinks we took a stage back to Pennsylvania. At the time, I wasn't sure I was expecting so I didn't want to worry him about the possibility. We were newly wed. I just couldn't bear to be so far away from him during this time, so that's why Laura and I stayed here. And now I'm glad we did. Promise you won't breathe a word, Nessa."

Nessa felt honored to be trusted by the sisters and was happy their friendship was getting off to a good start.

"I promise," she said.

CHAPTER SIX

A Terrible Mistake

Nessa carried the sisters' secret close to her heart. She wanted them to trust her.

But she wasn't sure why a baby coming needed to be a secret, unless what the whispering ladies had said was true. Nessa wondered if the reason the lieutenant had sent Fanny Jo away was because he wanted a divorce.

The next day, Nessa stood with Mrs. Lockett at a table beneath the kitchen window, scrubbing breakfast dishes. Mrs. Lockett asked about her visit. Suddenly, Nessa felt miserable. Keeping a secret wasn't as easy as she thought it would be. It was hard to talk about the sisters without revealing the news.

". . . and did Laura like the strawberries?" asked Mrs. Lockett. She handed Nessa a plate to dry.

Nessa took a dish towel and carefully rubbed the surface and rim. "Oh, yes, she truly did."

"Wonderful," continued Mrs. Lockett. "Laura told me that every summer their father had a strawberry patch and there was always enough to feed their neighborhood twice over. It sounds so lovely I don't blame 'em for being homesick. And how was Fanny Jo feelin'?"

"I reckon she's as well as can be expected."

Mrs. Lockett went to the stove for the kettle, then poured more steaming water into the dishpan. "Whatever do you mean, Nessa? She ain't sick with typhoid or anything like that, I hope?"

"No, nothing like that," Nessa quickly replied. "The weather's just too hot for her, is all."

"Very well, dear, when we finish here would you mind going to Filmore's for me? A wagon came in yesterday with crates of canned pineapple and canned lobster. It's quite exotic, but I want to try something different for supper tonight. Put it on my account as usual."

Nessa hung up her apron behind the kitchen door, eager for this errand. Mr. Filmore was her favorite sutler. He and his daughter, Ivy, had arrived at Fort Larned some weeks after Nessa and were well liked by all. She and Ivy were the same age.

Mr. Filmore's store was similar to the Applewoods'. Because lumber was scarce, it was built from strips of sod, layer upon layer. It still seemed funny to Nessa to see grass sticking out of the brown walls, and grass growing on a roof, though it was a common sight in Kansas. Within Mr. Filmore's compound was their sod house, a corral, a seamstress shop, and another building where soldiers could play cards or billiards when off duty. He planned to put in a bowling alley for them as soon as his shipment of balls and pins arrived from the East.

The aroma of nutmeg and fresh-ground coffee greeted Nessa when she walked in the door. Shelves lined the walls, bulging with bolts of cloth, blankets, pots, pans, and candles. Hanging from the low ceiling were sides of smoked ham and bacon covered in netting, sticks of salami, and clusters of small white onions. Inside a glass case was a colorful display of thimbles and hat pins. Nessa loved coming here.

"How nice to see you, sweetheart," said Mr. Filmore. "Ivy," he called into a storeroom, "Nessa's here. And what shall it be today?"

Nessa handed him the list from Mrs. Lockett.

Ivy came from behind a curtain carrying a tiny box of sewing needles and began arranging them inside the case. Her brown hair was in braids down her back, tied with yellow ribbons.

"I'm so glad you're here, Nessa. We heard about your new horse. Can I see him?"

"Oh, yes. When you're done here, come home with me." Nessa liked the girl's scuffed shoes and that she wasn't fancied up. Her calico dress was patched in places and short at the wrists. Not only did Nessa like that they were dressed similarly, but Nessa also felt tender toward Ivy because she, too, had suffered loss. Her mother and sisters had died the summer before of cholera. As soon as their graves were covered with dirt, Ivy's father moved them here to start a new life.

Even though Ivy had shared this heartbreak with Nessa, Nessa had yet to reveal anything about herself except that she had come from an orphanage. So far she had trusted only one person with the troubling details of why she had fled Independence — Mrs. Lockett. Nessa worried if other people knew about Reverend McDuff, they'd have one more reason not to trust her.

While whistling a happy tune, Mr. Filmore packed a basket. In went six cans of lobster, three of pineapple, a bottle of tomato catsup, a sack of cornmeal, and a small box of crackers. It was heavy. The girls lifted it between them, each holding a side of the handle.

"Bye, Papa," called Ivy. When they were outside, she said to Nessa, "I saw you going to the sisters' yesterday. Are they well? I heard Fanny Jo's a bit blue."

"They're fine," replied Nessa. The secret burned inside her. They continued along the creek toward the boardinghouse. "I know what," she said, "let's sit here for a while and cool off."

The spreading branches of an elm tree shaded the cove where they waded. Minnows darted through the clear water, and a small leopard frog hopped out of their way. Mosquitoes swarmed over the surface. Nessa splashed at them, then splashed her face and neck to cool off. She pictured Fanny Jo in her smothering hot cabin.

"What're you thinking about?" asked Ivy. Her brown eyes were kind. Freckles covered her nose and cheeks.

Nessa sighed. "I feel sorry for Fanny Jo," she said.

"How come?"

Nessa's heart beat fast. She had promised not to tell anyone, but Fanny Jo's news was boiling inside her. Nessa wondered if Ivy would understand how much she wanted to be her friend if she confided in her.

"Well," began Nessa, "Fanny Jo's expecting a baby, but her husband left her and if her father the senator finds out, he'll disown her and it will be a disgrace to the family. They're acquaintances with President Johnson in Washington. . . ."

Suddenly, Nessa felt so ashamed of the story she had blurted out and so prickled by the mosquitoes, she jumped in the river. Underwater, she opened her eyes. Everything was blurry, but as she rolled in the current she could see Ivy's bare feet in the sand, surrounded by minnows. She came up for air, her braids and dress dripping wet. Though she was cooler, she felt worse than before. If only she had dunked herself first, maybe she would still have the secret inside her.

Ivy's eyes were big. "Is it true?" she asked. "What you just said about Fanny Jo?"

Nessa nodded.

Ivy looked toward Suds Row. "No wonder she's so sad."

The wind blew hot against Nessa's wet dress as they continued along the path. Her hair was nearly dry by the time they carried the basket onto the porch and into the steamy kitchen. To herself she vowed that from now on she would guard Fanny Jo's news in earnest and not tell another soul.

"Hello, girls," said Mrs. Lockett. "And thank you so much. Set it on the table here. I was just beatin' some eggs for a nice chocolate cake. Do you want to sift the flour for me?"

Ivy took one of the extra aprons hanging from pegs by the door and tied it over her neck and around her waist.

"Mrs. Lockett," she said, "did you know Fanny Jo's husband doesn't want her anymore, plus she's going to have a baby and her father the senator will lose his position in Washington because of the disgrace. . . ."

Nessa's mouth dropped open. She didn't know what to say.

Mrs. Lockett set her whisk down on the table and looked at the girls. "My word, Ivy, is this true?"

"Yes, ma'am."

"But where did you ever hear such a thing?"

Ivy glanced at Nessa, then down at the floor.

In a small voice Ivy said, "I just heard it, is all."

CHAPTER SEVEN

Broken Fence

Nessa's ears burned as Mrs. Lockett questioned Ivy.

"I'm disappointed you would gossip like this, Ivy," she said. "Do you reckon how words can hurt, especially if they're false?"

Ivy swallowed hard. Her face was already red from the heat of the kitchen, but Nessa was sure the color rising in Ivy's cheeks was from Mrs. Lockett's scolding.

"As for you, Nessa," she said, "I pray this information stays between us and that you won't breathe a word to no one. If any of this is true, it's Fanny Jo's story to tell, it ain't ours." She turned to the cupboard and pulled out a burlap sack of flour.

"Six cups into that bowl, please, Nessa. Ivy, the tub of butter is under the floorboards there in the pantry. I'll need two cups, please."

Mrs. Lockett's jaw was tight. Nessa had never before seen her angry. As the woman beat the eggs in its bowl, Nessa noticed her strong arms where the sleeves were rolled up.

"My word," she said again. Some minutes later, Mrs.

Lockett looked up from the bowl now brimming with yellow foam. "Ivy dear, the worst kind of gossip is when we repeat things we've heard *others* say. We can't be sure if what they are sayin' is true, or what their reason is behind even sayin' it in the first place."

Ivy kept her eyes lowered. "Yes, ma'am," she said.

Nessa felt so hot she thought she might faint. She couldn't bring herself to look at Ivy or Mrs. Lockett. Slowly, she measured the flour cup by cup into the large wooden bowl. From the parlor came the sound of a clock chiming.

It was only ten o'clock in the morning and already Nessa was in trouble.

The girls were silent during the rest of the cake preparation. When Mrs. Lockett slid the three circular pans into the oven, Ivy took off her apron.

"I have to go help Papa now," she said. Without saying good-bye to Nessa, she hurried out the back door.

Mrs. Lockett wiped her brow with her sleeve then looked at Nessa, who was staring out the window at her friend. "Is there somethin' you want to tell me, honey?"

Nessa shook her head. She stood by the table, wondering how everything had gotten so mixed up. Then the worst happened.

A gentleman guest and his wife came into the kitchen from the parlor. Nessa remembered seeing them there earlier, reading. She now realized they had heard the entire conversation.

"We're going out for some fresh air, madam," they said to Mrs. Lockett. "When will you be serving lunch?"

"I'll be ringin' the bell at noon," she said.

The man tipped his hat, then escorted his wife outside.

Nessa and Mrs. Lockett watched through the open door as the couple headed toward town. The man and woman had their heads turned toward each other in conversation.

"True or not," said Mrs. Lockett, "Fanny Jo's story is gonna reach other ears, then— "

"Oh, it's all my fault," Nessa burst out. "I didn't mean to tell, and now it's a terrible mess. A while back, I overheard the seamstress and some ladies talking. Fanny Jo told me about the baby, but that's all she said. Now she'll hate me for breaking my promise. Ivy's mad at me, too. Oh, I just wanted to be their friends."

Mrs. Lockett lifted a sack of turnips she'd brought up from the root cellar and dumped them on the table. With a knife she began peeling away the rough skins. "Cut these, please, into quarters, Nessa, then put them into the kettle. Water's almost boilin'." She looked at Nessa's face and her moist eyes.

"My dear," she said, "if someone broke the fence to our corral and your little colt got loose, it would take some amount of searchin' and runnin' to bring him back. And until the fence was fixed, the same thing would happen all over again and who knows where he might get to? You might lose 'im forever."

Nessa looked up at Mrs. Lockett. "What do you mean?" Her voice trembled.

The woman dabbed a dish towel against Nessa's wet cheeks. "You must mend what's broken, Nessa. First say you're sorry to God and mean it. Then ask for His wisdom. He'll show you what to do." She cupped Nessa's chin. "And in the future, don't ever repeat two words you overhear in that seamstress shop."

While cutting the turnips, Nessa was quiet. She savored the soothing aroma of the cake baking as she watched Mrs. Lockett move through the kitchen with purpose.

Oh, Jesus, she prayed silently, *I'm so sorry for giving away Fanny Jo's secret, for assuming I knew the whole story. And for letting Ivy take the blame . . . please show me what to do, how to fix this trouble.*

She took in the sight of Minnie coming up from the creek with a pail of water. Rolly was leading his horse and cart into the yard. It was piled with buffalo chips, the dried dung that would feed the cooking fires. How Nessa cherished these children, as if they were her true sister and brother.

But she was ashamed of herself. What kind of example was she setting, to repeat a story without learning if it was true? And how could she call herself a friend if she couldn't be trusted?

She carried the bowl of turnips to the stove, poured them into the steaming water, then covered the kettle with its heavy iron lid.

As she did so, an idea came to her.

"Mrs. Lockett," she said, "do you mind if I come back later to mash the turnips? There's something I need to do."

Mrs. Lockett was pulling the cake pans from the oven. She set them in the wide windowsill, then smiled at Nessa.

"Take your time, dear."

Nessa hurried along the path to Filmore's and was out of breath when she stepped into the store.

"Mr. Filmore," she said, "I'm here to see Ivy, please."

He looked at her with sadness. "I'm sorry, Nessa, she doesn't want to see you."

"But, sir, it's important —"

"She said she doesn't want to see you."

CHAPTER EIGHT

A Fine Leather Shoe

Nessa left Mr. Filmore's, choking back tears. It was all her fault. How could she have let Ivy stand there and take Mrs. Lockett's scolding without coming to her rescue? It was worse than telling a lie. No wonder Ivy wouldn't talk to her.

She wondered now if they would ever become friends.

It was too hot to hide herself away upstairs in her room, and it was too hot to walk out to the cemetery where she could really be alone. Her chest ached with all the tears building up inside. But there was no time to cry. She must go to Fanny Jo and tell her everything.

This time she walked the long way around the fort. At this moment, Nessa lacked the courage to take the sidewalk on Officers' Row. She couldn't bear to be reprimanded again today. She passed the blacksmith and library, then the sail maker. Here two men were busy sewing a large sheet of canvas for a wagon cover.

As she rounded the corner by the carpenter's tent, she saw something that made her heart sink. Laura was coming out of the Applewoods' store. The door was open.

Behind her came the man and woman from the board-inghouse. They were chatting with two ladies finely dressed in hoopskirts and carrying parasols that they opened as soon as they stepped out into the hot sun.

Laura walked briskly across the parade ground, cut through a path between the soldiers' barracks, then out to the grassy area of Suds Row.

Nessa waited in the shade of the tent. When she realized she wouldn't be able to make it to the sisters' hut before Laura, she sat down in the dirt.

I've really made a mess of things, Lord. What now? She closed her eyes to gather her thoughts. After a moment something nudged her knee. Nessa looked down. Her yellow puppy had followed her, carrying something in her mouth all the way from home.

"Drop it, Green." She used the phrase she'd been practicing. Nearly every day Green brought something from somewhere to show Nessa. Yesterday it was a ball of yarn from Mrs. Lockett's knitting basket. Last evening it was a gentleman's pipe.

"Drop it," she said again, in a deeper voice. After a moment, a man's fine leather shoe fell to the grass.

"Oh, no. Where'd you get this, you naughty girl?" Nessa turned it over in her hand, trying to remember where she'd seen it and guessed it must belong to one of Mrs. Lockett's boarders.

Nessa's shoulders sagged. That's all she needed now, was for someone to accuse her of being a thief. She looked in the direction of the boardinghouse, wondering if she should hurry back with the stolen item or visit

Fanny Jo. The sun was nearly overhead, and soon Mrs. Lockett would be ringing the dinner bell.

Well, first things first, she thought, on her way to Suds Row. She stared at the sisters' cabin, wondering what to say. Green meanwhile found a sliver of shade and lay down with her head on her paws. She cast a sympathetic eye toward her mistress.

Fanny Jo opened the door before Nessa had a chance to knock. Her hair was combed up in an elegant swirl, her brow and neck damp from the heat. The cut of her dress was loose, not pinched in by a corset. To Nessa she looked beautiful, but her eyes flashed with anger.

"I trusted you, Nessa. I thought we were friends." Fanny Jo raised her hands in exasperation. "The reason I didn't announce my personal life to the whole world was because I first wanted to tell my husband. Laura and I were going to make the trip to Fort Dodge this week. But now, he'll no doubt hear it from one of the soldiers."

"I . . . Oh, dear . . . Fanny Jo, I made a terrible mistake."

"Indeed you did. The rumors spoken to Laura are just dreadful. I'm hurt you didn't first come to me so we could have talked. I don't know why you would have thought such things."

Nessa could see Laura inside by the window. Sunlight against her face showed she had been crying. She would not look at Nessa.

"When we were on the stagecoach," Fanny Jo continued, "do you recall us telling you how our brother Jimmy was killed in the Battle of Gettysburg, and about our older brother Ben? How he starved to death in Andersonville prison? Our parents are beside themselves with grief, which is why they weren't pleased we traveled so far from home. Now I have no idea how they will react to this. Not that any of this is your business." She fanned herself with a magazine.

Nessa hung her head. "I'm so sorry, Fanny Jo. Please forgive me." Without waiting for a response, she turned for the path and hurried home along the creek, still carrying the man's shoe, Green loping beside her.

Mrs. Lockett was on the back porch, rinsing eggs from the henhouse in a pail of water.

"Well?" she asked.

Nessa sat on the steps. She brushed at the mosquitoes settling on her arms. "I did what you said, Mrs. Lockett, but I don't think God has forgiven me. Nothing's turned out like I hoped. Fanny Jo and Laura are furious, and Ivy won't even speak to me. I don't blame them, though."

"Hmm," said Mrs. Lockett. She set each egg in her basket, then poured the water over the railing into the lilac bush.

"Nessa, when we ask God to forgive us, from the bottom of our hearts, He does. As far as the East is from the West, that's how far He removes our transgressions from us, that's what the Bible says. He don't keep track of our mistakes, and we shouldn't, neither. I'm sure our good Lord has forgiven you, dear, but forgiveness ain't always followed right away by happiness. Some folks feel a hurt so deeply, it takes them a long time to forgive."

Nessa gazed out over the prairie where shivery waves

of heat looked like water. A streak of dark blue clouds hinted at rain. How Nessa wished the sky would thunder and pour down on the hot land. How she wished the blistering wind would turn cool.

If God had truly forgiven her, why did she feel so bad?

Mrs. Lockett stood up to carry the eggs inside. She handed the dinner bell to Nessa. "Ring it in ten minutes, honey. I'll finish up the gravy, meantime. Say, what's that you got there?" She nodded toward the shoe.

Nessa sighed. "I was hoping you'd know who it belongs to. Green stole it."

Mrs. Lockett smiled. "Quick-like, Nessa, take it upstairs, second room, the gentleman was lookin' high and low for it this mornin'. Seems he left his shoes outside his door last night believin' we'd clean 'em by breakfast, imagine that. As if we girls ain't got nothin' better to do."

CHAPTER NINE

———◆———

The Blacksmith

Nessa got up earlier than usual. From her open window she could hear the bugler at the fort, playing reveille. *It's time to get up. It's time to get up!* Dawn was turning the sky bright blue when she went outside to feed Wildwing. The colt whinnied when he saw her and walked excitedly over to the fence, tripping over his long hoof.

"Good boy," she said, letting herself into the corral. She leaned down to feel his withers against her cheek and stroked his square jaw.

"I'm so glad you're still my friend," she told him. "Fanny Jo is furious with me and so is Laura. Ivy refused to see me when I went to apologize." Nessa continued to tell Wildwing about her embarrassing mistake while grooming his dusty back with a brush. Tears choked her throat.

". . . and Mr. Applewood doesn't like me. Everyone's just waiting for me to make a mistake with the students so they can get rid of me." She hugged Wildwing again. She liked the way his spots freckled his gray flanks. "Oh, you're such a good horse." He watched her rake the soiled straw into a manure pile and add fresh hay under the lean-to, then followed her to the barn for oats. When she noticed his limp, she had a tender thought.

"I'm glad you aren't perfect, Wildwing, or else you'd be working for the army and would be in danger on the trail. Maybe when you're older and if your hoof is better, I can ride you to school, then we can let the children ride you, too, for a special treat after they do their lessons."

Three times she took her bucket to the creek to fill the water trough. On the fourth trip, she washed her face and hands in the cold stream. It was her favorite time of day. Everything seemed fresh and hopeful. The air was balmy, the sky now pale pink from the sun that would rise any moment. A dove cooed from its perch on the fence, then another answered from the roof of the barn.

Before latching the corral gate, she again petted her colt's velvety nose. "And guess what else?" she said. "This afternoon, Rolly and I are taking you to meet someone special."

Rolly stood in the stone doorway of the blacksmith's shop while Nessa stayed outside with Wildwing. There were several smithies at the fort, many who worked out of tents, but Mr. Bell was her favorite. He and his wife were friends of Mrs. Lockett. Several times after church, the Bells had driven Minnie and Nessa to their dugout along the river to enjoy supper together.

"'Afternoon, Nessa," Mr. Bell called to her over the roar of bellows. "Hello there, son. Give me a minute and

I'll be right out." With a pair of long-handle iron tongs, he lifted a glowing red bar from the flames of his fire. It looked like a short stick until he began hammering it into the shape of an oval. Before the orb was closed, Mr. Bell joined it with another oval, linking the two with one sharp blow of his hammer. Nessa realized he was making a chain.

"Leg irons," he said with a laugh. "For the stockade. There're two prisoners there right now who don't know how to salute an officer." He dipped the tongs into a barrel of water. A hiss of steam rose into the hot air as the iron links cooled.

"Well, let's see what we got here, kids," he said, coming out into the sunlight. Mr. Bell's sleeves were rolled above his elbows and the hair was singed off his muscular arms. He stroked Wildwing's fuzzy ears. "My, my. Sure is a handsome little fella."

While Nessa held the rope, Mr. Bell kneeled alongside the colt, facing its tail. As he leaned into his flank, he gently lifted the misshapen front hoof.

"And the soldier was going to shoot 'im," Rolly explained about the rescue.

"Well, son," said Mr. Bell, "the army doesn't have a lot of time to fuss with animals that aren't going to be useful. But I'll tell you what . . ." He stood up and disappeared into the dark shop, returning a moment later holding a small tool. "If you file Wildwing's hoof as it grows — oh, say, once a week — it might, and I say *might*, begin to turn properly in four to six months. Clean his feet every day with water and a cloth, because it looks like he's also got a sore of some kind, maybe thrush. Be gentle as can be, though, because his foot is hurting him, see?"

Mr. Bell knelt again and pressed his thumb into the soft underside of the lifted hoof. Wildwing flinched backward and tossed his head.

"It's all right, boy," he said, patting the colt's side. "Your friends here are gonna take good care of you."

On the first day of school, Nessa hurried to help Mrs. Lockett with breakfast. She set eight bowls of porridge on the table, cut the corn bread into squares, and put out a plate of butter. The pitcher of fresh cream was from Rolly's milking last evening. Coffee was warming on the stove, ready to be served.

But Nessa was too excited to eat and instead just pushed her spoon around in her bowl until everyone had finished. After she dried and put away the breakfast dishes, she rushed upstairs for one last thing.

In her trunk was a hatbox. She lifted the round lid and pulled out a crisp yellow hat, trimmed with black velvet. Nessa stood in front of her mirror, positioning it on her head. The brim curved gracefully over one cheek and reminded her of a pretty sunflower. She imagined that her mother had worn this to church or to an important meeting.

If only she could see me now, Nessa thought, *a schoolteacher with a proper hat.*

Out the kitchen door she went, carrying her Bible in one hand and lunch pail in the other. Minnie and Rolly followed, for the path to the schoolhouse was narrow. The tall bluestem grasses on either side were wet with morning dew, and even brushing against them soaked their shoes and stockings. Green ran ahead, then burst into a clearing after a black-tailed jackrabbit. The melodic songs of meadowlarks and chickadees filled the air. Prairie dogs trilled warnings to one another upon the children's approach.

In the back of her mind, Nessa pictured the Indian boy and wondered if he was nearby. The idea made her nervous, but she remembered he hadn't hurt her. She also felt unsettled about facing her class for the first time since last term. Would there be any new students? Would Ivy come? And if Big Howard were there, would he cause difficulties again?

Oh, well, thought Nessa, *no matter what happens, today is a new day.* She lifted her chin to smell the air. It was a beautiful morning. The wind carried the pleasant scent of horses and oxen from corrals at the fort.

And Mr. Bell's news about Wildwing had filled her with hope.

CHAPTER TEN

School Begins

The schoolhouse where Nessa taught last term was a mile from town and formerly had been a storage building on Mr. Button's ranch. He and his cousin had carved windows into the sod walls and installed a wood-burning stove for when the weather turned cold. They had built benches with desks for the students and a small oak table for the teacher. The outhouse had a low seat with a hole that was on the small side so none of the students would fall in.

Mr. Button had been on the step when Nessa arrived, and followed her inside. His thick mustache moved over his cheeks as he smiled. Blue suspenders held up his trousers over his huge belly, and Nessa noticed evidence of his breakfast on his shirt: bread crumbs and spots of egg. As always, his fingers were stained with ink from setting type for his newspaper.

"'Morning, Miss Vanessa," he said, beaming with pride at her. "You'll find fresh paper on your desk, left over from last week's news, blank on one side. The pencils, I got 'em from the carpenter, and the McGuffey readers you ordered should be coming with one of the next freight teams." He leaned close to whisper. The smell of coffee was on his breath. "Got a little surprise for you, Nessa."

He pulled a small sack from his pocket and handed it to her. "Peppermints for the children."

"Oh, thank you so much, Mr. Button." She took the bag and smiled. It was actually one of Mr. Button's old socks, patched in the toe and heel. Bits of grass were poking out of the yarn as if he had never washed it. "This is very thoughtful of you, thank you," she said again. By now she was used to the peculiar way he shared things and no longer felt squeamish.

"Well, then," said Mr. Button, brushing his hands together, "guess I'll get to work myself, two new stories to print up. The other night some soldiers came down sick with fever and chills, maybe from something they ate. The surgeon says it doesn't appear to be contagious, but he hopes to high heaven it's not typhoid. Other story is the Indians. A rancher not far from here lost all his stock and had his barn burned to the ground. Keep careful watch now, Nessa. I'll be looking out for you, too, and the cavalry's on alert."

Nessa had his warning in mind as she made her way to her desk.

Nessa stood in the front of the class, regarding her students. She was pleased to see Big Howard in the back row sitting quietly next to Rolly. He was taller than Nessa, with the strong thick arms of a boy who works hard on his father's ranch. At the start of last term he had made trouble for Nessa and refused to do his lessons, but over the summer she had noticed a pleasant change. He regularly watered Peter's tree at the cemetery and often asked Nessa when school was going to resume.

"Good morning, class." She smiled and spoke each child's name. In the middle row were Lucy and Augusta, both nine years old and swinging their feet with the fidgets, and Minnie. In the front row where Peter had sat were two new students. A boy of eight, who had whitish-blond hair and sunburned cheeks, introduced himself as Sven.

Next to him was a smaller girl with hair the color of pumpkin, in a mop of curls. She was Peter's younger sister, Poppy.

With a lump in her throat, Nessa swallowed back the memory of the summer's sad events.

"I'm happy to see all of you," said Nessa. "Poppy, can you tell the class how old you are?"

The girl's hands were folded in her lap. She sat very still. "Five," she whispered. After a moment, she reached inside the sash of her dress and took out a small envelope. "For you, Teacher," she said.

Nessa took the letter and walked over to a window where sunlight slanted in over the sill. "Excuse me a moment, boys and girls," she said. Carefully, she broke the wax seal and unfolded the stationery. She hesitated. The letter Mrs. Sullivan wrote after Peter's death had surprised her with its kindness. The family did not blame her for the rattlesnake that had killed their son.

Still, Nessa's heart fluttered wondering what this letter might say.

Dear Nessa,

Poppy's birthday was yesterday. When she blew out the five candles on her cake we asked what she had wished for. "To go to school like Peter," she answered. She remembers how much her brother liked you. Lieutenant Sullivan and I know you're a good teacher and that Poppy will come to love learning as much as our son did.
Sincerely,
Mrs. Sullivan

Nessa looked out the window at the wide blue sky. Her heart melted. She wanted to cry, but of course would not allow herself in front of her students. It was an honor to be trusted with these children, especially by Peter's parents. The fears she had confided earlier to Wildwing were being replaced with confidence. She breathed a silent prayer.

Thank You again, Lord, for leading me to Prairie River. Please show me today what to do and how to do it. Then she remembered another missing student.

Ivy.

Dear Jesus, please help me be a friend to Ivy. Help me repair the mistakes I made with her, and the sisters, too. Please help me earn another chance.

CHAPTER ELEVEN

A Curious Visitor

*N*essa began each school day by reading from her Bible, as Miss Eva had done in the orphanage. It was much smaller than the one she had discovered in her trunk, the one stamped with her father's name, Howard L. Clemens.

Hers fit in the palm of her hand and was bound in red leather. She didn't recall who had given it to her or upon what occasion. She just remembered always having it.

"*Psalm One hundred–three,*" she began reading aloud. "*Bless the Lord, O my soul; and all that is within me, bless His holy name. . . . For as the heaven is high above the earth, so great is His mercy toward them that fear Him; As far as the east is from the west, so far hath He removed our transgressions from us.*"

Last night, Mrs. Lockett had shown her where to find this verse. Nessa was still distressed about the trouble she had caused and realized it would take time to earn back the friendships begun with Ivy, Fanny Jo, and Laura. But a peace had settled inside her. She believed with all her heart that God had, indeed, forgiven her mistakes and was not holding a grudge against her. This peace helped her concentrate on teaching.

During the second week of school, the thermometer hovered above ninety degrees in the shade. One hot morning, Nessa opened the door to help the wind move through the room. Flies swarmed overhead and mosquitoes caused much hand slapping and waving. Nessa had called both Augusta and Sven to her desk to help correct their spelling. Meanwhile, Green slept through all the commotion at her feet.

Nessa noticed Poppy had left her seat and stood at the window, staring out. She didn't want to scold her youngest student because she was only five and had been sitting quietly the past hour.

"Poppy?" she asked. "Would you like to come up by me, and I'll read to you?"

The child didn't answer.

Another minute passed. Nessa wasn't sure what to do. Then she heard a small voice.

"Teacher?" Poppy pointed outside.

Suddenly, the window grew dark, as if a shade had been drawn. Nessa was so startled, she hurried over to Poppy to pull her away. Just then the building shook.

A cry of surprise came from her students.

"It's all right," Nessa told them, but she noticed her own mouth had gone dry. *Are Indians attacking?*

The windows rattled as the shaking continued, then once again sunshine filled the room as the dark object moved away.

Nessa looked out and was relieved to see it was just a large buffalo. Its brown fur was shaggy, with balls of mud dangling from its belly and neck. Bare patches were along its sides, as if it was shedding. Its enormous head turned toward her, a brown eye looking inside the schoolhouse.

"Shoo!" Nessa yelled through the glass. "Go away!" She remembered seeing a small herd by the river that morning and wondered why this bull had strayed.

But instead of leaving, the animal threw its weight against the wall with a thud.

"Oh, no," said Rolly. "He's a stubborn old fella. I think he's scratching his back."

A sound of dirt sprinkling onto the floor drew Nessa's eyes to the corner. A narrow shaft of sunlight shone in through a crack that hadn't been there before.

The wall was moving.

"We have to make him leave," said Nessa. "Come on, Rolly."

Howard stood up. "Wait, Miss Nessa. I'll go to town for help. You shouldn't go near such a big buffalo. He could hurt you."

Nessa hesitated. Another thump to the wall brought a fresh splash of dirt. To her horror, the crack had widened and more daylight showed through. She felt her heart in her throat, but tried to stay calm. In a measured voice she said, "That's very kind of you, Howard, but there isn't enough time. Children, you stay here and hold tight to Green, do not let her follow me. Howard is in charge."

Outside, Nessa peered around the corner to look at

the animal. A strong musky odor reached her. It was taller than a man and as wide as a wagon. Its mouth was open as it panted under the warm sun. At the sight of its bloated tongue, Nessa wondered why soldiers considered it a delicacy to eat.

"Skedaddle!" she yelled, trying out the word she had heard the soldier use.

Rolly put a reassuring hand on her arm. "Watch this," he said. With a dramatic wave, he held up his slingshot and positioned a rock in its leather pouch. As he took aim, he gave Nessa a confident smile, pulled back the sinewy string, then released it.

A small puff of dust rose from the animal's side. Unfazed by the hit, it continued to rub its head against the sod bricks.

"Drat," he said, bending down for another stone. "I'll get 'im this time. Watch, Nessa."

Rolly's next shot landed in the dirt. The next flew over the animal's back and onto the roof of the schoolhouse. When his fourth attempt struck the wall, barely missing the window, Nessa decided to do something herself.

She lifted her hem and ran toward the bull, flapping her petticoat and screaming, "Shoo!" She knew it wasn't ladylike, but she worried the wall might cave in, and it was her job to protect the children. As she got closer, she stomped her feet and clapped her hands. "Shoo now. . . . Go home. . . . Skedaddle!"

The buffalo turned his gaze to Nessa. Bits of grass were stuck to his moist nose. He shook his massive head back and forth as if trying to get a good look at her, then began to back up. "Shoo!" Nessa charged at him again, this time getting even closer. With that, the whites of his eyes flashed and he turned away. His hooves looked like tiny black shoes on sticks as he ambled away.

Rolly ran up to Nessa, pointing his slingshot at the departing visitor. "I can't believe you just did that," he said. "That old bull coulda knocked you down and stepped on you before I could stop 'im, Nessa. Woo-ee, he was a big one. Did you see how his teeth were black and rotting? Boy, did he stink. Wait'll I tell Mother."

On the way home from school, Minnie held Nessa's hand. With the sun at their backs, they walked on their shadows with each step. "Nessa?" she asked. "What would you have done if that buffalo pushed down the wall?"

Nessa laughed. "I have no idea! One thing is for sure, we all could have gone home early."

Minnie smiled up at her. "When my papa gets back from the war, he's gonna be glad to meet you, Nessa. I know he'll like you."

After supper, Mr. Applewood stood on the front porch, talking to Mrs. Lockett. His voice was loud and angry. Nessa couldn't see him, but she could hear him from the open window as she washed dishes.

"Furthermore," he said, "the committee questions her judgment. As teacher, she should have run to the fort and gotten some of the men to help. I don't think we can trust her with the children. Folks are talking all up and down about how foolish she is, how a bull roaming around by himself like that is either rabid or mad. She never should have challenged it."

Mrs. Lockett's voice was so gentle, Nessa strained to listen, standing perfectly still so she could hear better. Nessa pressed her wet hands against her apron to silence the dripping water.

"Now, now, Tom," the woman said from outside, "you know plain as I do that those children could have been in danger if she left 'em to get help. And what then? You still would've found a reason to wag your finger in Nessa's face. Leave the poor girl alone. Her heart's pure gold. Now're you stayin' for a cup of coffee or not? I got fresh cream and some berry pie to go with it."

Nessa didn't hear the man's response, but she did hear his footsteps as he left the porch. Suddenly, she felt exhausted by the day's events. It seemed that no matter what she did, someone would be mad at her for something.

She was glad Mr. Applewood didn't come into the kitchen for coffee.

CHAPTER TWELVE

————⊷◆⊶————

Harvest

As the nights grew cooler, Nessa knew frost would soon freeze the earth. She instructed her students to bring baskets to school so they could finish harvesting the garden they had planted in the spring.

"We'll spend the entire day outside," she announced to a happy eruption. "Lessons will be on everything we see and touch, so, girls, wear an old apron over your dresses. Boys, we'll need shovels, and, Rolly, it would be a big help if you could bring your cart, too."

The garden was near the school, on the other side of the creek. They had planted seeds gathered in town from families and some of the soldiers' wives. Since Nessa hadn't kept track of what was to be a vegetable, flower, or fruit, the garden had burst into a wild display of color and shape. Sunflowers and hollyhocks had towered over rows of poppies, daisies, and radishes. Melons and beans had trailed on vines running between berry bushes.

"An exuberant garden," Mr. Button had called it.

The children had faithfully carried water from the stream in their pails, much of it sloshing over as they walked. As a result, during summer the path had sprouted wildflowers.

Most of what remained now was squash, small orange pumpkins, and a variety of cucumbers perfect for making gherkins.

As the children filled their arms, Nessa had them count how many items they picked up, then add in their heads the totals, and then they took turns subtracting from one another's baskets. She quizzed them on the animal tracks and insects they found crawling in the dirt, ever mindful to beware of snakes. They called out names of geese and sandhill cranes winging overhead, even the noisy blue jays and a distant warble of turkeys. From the creek, they heard the rapid patter of a woodpecker. When it flew to another tree, they were able to see its crimson head and crimson throat, the underside of its wings a vivid white and black. The sight of such a handsome bird filled Nessa with happiness. It reminded her of how Miss Eva had taken her on walks through the streets of Independence, pointing out every beautiful living creature.

Nessa was grateful for her former teacher. Now there was so much she wanted to show her own students.

Rolly loaded pumpkins into his cart, for they were too heavy to carry and the children's baskets were already full.

"Thank you, Rolly," she said as he left for town with the new boy, Sven, sitting next to him; Big Howard was in back. "We'll meet you at the Applewoods' so we can share some of our harvest with them." Nessa was shocked that she had thought to do something nice for the couple, but then remembered what she had read the night before in her father's Bible. He had underlined passages in the Book of Luke in which Jesus said you should treat people the way you want them to treat you. In this passage, Jesus also said if you only love those who love you, what credit is that to you? Even sinners love those who love them.

Nessa wondered why her father had written *AMEN!* in the margin. As she searched to know more about him, she kept reading and studying the sections he marked. If they had been important to him, maybe they were principles he would have wanted her to learn, too.

Nessa recalled when she had recently taken Mrs. Applewood a bouquet of daisies. Doing so had made Nessa feel happy, but it hadn't seemed to make the woman like her any better. Truth was, it was hard for Nessa to be nice to the storekeepers when they continued to treat her harshly. She didn't think she would ever be able to love them.

But Nessa wanted to follow the words of Jesus. Thinking further on the matter, she realized it would mean a lot to her if someone brought *her* a basket of colorful things from a garden.

Since that's how *she* would like to be treated, she would do the same for Mr. and Mrs. Applewood.

More than anything, Nessa wanted to do something nice for Ivy. She gathered an armful of sweet-smelling sage and tied the stems together with a ribbon from her hair.

As Nessa walked with her students toward the fort, arms laden with baskets, she kept glancing around, to keep an eye on each child. She didn't want any of them to wander off as Peter had.

But out of the corner of her eye, something caught her attention. A figure on horseback, riding along the top of a ravine. The pony was chocolate-brown. Fluttering from its forelock was a white feather.

She picked up the pace without letting the children know that she was hurrying. Another glance backward and there were now three on horseback. The wind was blowing the manes and tails.

Nessa's heart beat fast. She again reminded herself the Indian boy hadn't chased her after they had seen each other in the cemetery. Still, she felt anxious. The last thing she needed was to have a confrontation with Indians when she had taken the children off the school grounds. What would the townsfolk say then?

"Let's sing!" she cried, wanting a distraction. Her students knew the words to "The Modern Belle," for it was in the songbook she shared with them each afternoon. The words always made them laugh.

> *"The daughter sits in the parlor,*
> *And rocks in the easy chair.*
> *She is dress'd in her silks and satins,*
> *And jewels are in her hair.*
> *She smiles and she sniggles and simpers,*
> *And simpers and sniggles and winks,*
> *And although she talks but a little,*
> *'Tis mostly more than she thinks. . . ."*

By the time they finished the last verse, they had arrived at the edge of the sutlers' compound. She looked over her shoulder, and the horsemen had disappeared from sight. Rolly and the boys were already there with his full cart. Nessa took her own basket, arranged it nicely with colorful squash and cucumbers. Then Sven rolled a pumpkin out of the cart into her arms. His white-blond locks fell over his eyes as he bent over.

"Thank you, Sven," she said. "Now, who would like to help me carry these things inside?"

"Me!" said Augusta and Lucy.

"Me, too!" said Minnie.

Poppy raised her hand. In a soft voice she asked, "May I help you, Teacher?"

Nessa touched the top of Poppy's curly head. "Of course you may. Here." She gave the girl a small pumpkin that was the color of her hair, then one to Minnie. The basket, she handed to Lucy and Augusta for them to carry together.

"Follow me," she said.

Nessa stepped into the store, hopeful. She felt good about having something to give, even if the owners didn't like her.

Mr. Applewood was behind the counter slicing a wheel of white cheese speckled with blue. His sleeves were rolled above his elbows.

"What do you want?" he asked without looking up from his task. His tone of voice was so gruff, Nessa momentarily lost heart.

But Poppy came forward with her pumpkin, the curls on her head bouncing with her little steps.

"We brought you a present," she said, reaching to place her squash on the counter.

At the sound of her tiny voice, Mr. Applewood set down his knife and looked at her over the tops of his spectacles. His beard made him look stern. Nessa cringed inside, worried he might say something that would hurt the children's feelings.

Minnie then set her pumpkin next to Poppy's. Lucy and Augusta lifted their basket to the counter.

He stepped forward, wiping his hands on his apron. His eyes went from the pumpkins to the girls to the overflowing basket.

"I do declare," he said before returning to his work. He didn't thank them, but Nessa was sure she saw the hint of a smile beneath Mr. Applewood's beard as he looked at the young students.

CHAPTER THIRTEEN

Letter

Rolly and Big Howard left with Sven to deliver the other pumpkins to Suds Row while Nessa walked to Mr. Filmore's store with her bouquet. She hadn't meant for the girls to come with her because she had dismissed them from school earlier, but in they marched, along with Green.

Ivy was arranging cans of corn on a shelf when the commotion of four children and a puppy made her look up. She smiled at them and immediately reached into a large jar of candy.

"Licorice drops are free today," she said, handing each girl a black circle the size of a checker. "Hello, Nessa. Would you like one, too?"

Nessa was startled by Ivy's friendly gesture. "Oh, no thank you," she answered. "But, here, I picked these for you. I've been thinking about you, Ivy."

Then in a rush of hopeful words, Nessa whispered, "Ivy, please forgive me for that day. I never should have told Fanny Jo's secret, and I feel terrible about letting Mrs. Lockett scold you. I was wrong to just stand there, and I don't blame you if —"

"It's all right, Nessa," Ivy interrupted. "I'm not so mad anymore. Once I did the same thing to my sister, and she wouldn't speak to me for a whole week, but shortly after that she and my other sister and our mother — well, you know — by morning they were . . ." Ivy turned away.

Nessa didn't know what to say. The littler girls were quiet.

After a moment, Ivy wiped her eyes with the back of her hand, then looked up. "Nessa, I was fixin' to come over today after supper. I decided I didn't want anything awful to happen before we had a chance to make up. I'm glad you came by. Sure you don't want some licorice?"

"Yes, I do now," said Nessa. "Thank you."

"Oh, I almost forgot," said Ivy. "A stage came in an hour ago from Fort Zarah. Papa sorted the mail real quick because there wasn't much. Anyway, there's a letter for you. I'll go get it."

Nessa ran upstairs and flung open her windows. A breeze immediately cooled her room. Her heart was bursting with happiness. Ivy didn't hate her, Mr. Applewood had almost smiled, and now she had a letter. The careful handwriting on the envelope was Albert's.

Sweet Albert.

She sat on her bed and patted the quilt next to her as Green jumped up.

"It's from Albert, our old friend from Independence," she told her dog, stroking her silky ears. "He would just love you, Green. He always wanted a puppy, but Mr. Carey wouldn't let any of us have pets."

Dear Nessa,

   Things are good here at the *Gazette*. My boss, the editor, let me write a story about the Cooley boys who are now bothering folks in Missouri. One of them was hanged last week for shooting up a bank and three society ladies. They think maybe he did the killing of Mr. Smith, that schoolteacher in Prairie River before you. Well, here it is, in print, front page. . . .

A piece of newsprint was in the envelope. Nessa unfolded it and read. Albert's spelling was much improved since his last letter. She smiled, remembering his dark eyes and hair, always mussed with curls. He was taller than Nessa and thin. They'd come to the orphanage within a week of each other, when they were four years old. All these years, they had been friends.

How she missed him! It made her happy that Mr. Carey had apprenticed him to a kind man.

But as she continued reading, her heart sank. A chill ran through her as she was reminded of Mr. Carey's arrangement for her.

   . . . Pastor McDuff came in and paid for an advertisement. I didn't tell him one thing about you, Nessa, but he said he's going to find you anyhow. . . .

Drawing in a breath, Nessa read a second news clipping.

REWARD
INFORMATION WANTED ON
RUNAWAY ORPHAN, FEMALE, 14 YRS.
SEE THE REVEREND M.J. MCDUFF
SECOND STREET CHURCH

Suddenly, Nessa's good cheer drained from her, as if she'd been splashed with water. Reverend McDuff was still looking for her.

> . . . but don't worry, Nessa. If I hear he's on a stage heading to Prairie River, I will be on it, too. He'll be sorry to see me in his shadow. Take care of yourself out there in the middle of nowheres. I was sad to hear what happened to your littlest student, Peter. He's in a better place now, I do believe.
> Fond regards,
> Albert

Nessa lay back on her bed, pressing the page to her heart. Albert sounded taller than before, if such a thing were possible to sense from a letter. She felt the breeze coming in over her and watched the patterns of sunlight on her ceiling.

Here I am again, Lord, talking to You about this problem. If the preacher comes after me, I don't reckon I'll know what to do. Thank You for this beautiful day and that Ivy and I are going to be friends again and please watch over Albert.

Her prayer was full of yearnings and worries and hopes. She closed her eyes.

Suddenly, her room was dark, and Minnie was shaking her arm. "Supper's ready," she said. "Mama's called three times already."

CHAPTER FOURTEEN

───◆◆◆───

A Dirt Patch

The next day, Mr. Button rapped his knuckles against the open schoolhouse door as he walked up the steps.

"Pardon me, Miss Vanessa," he said. "My cousin and I finally got our new plow and we've come to turn under your garden before the ground freezes, so we were wondering if your students would like to help. Oh, that there's Hoss. He's only nineteen, but, boy, is he strong." He pointed to a young man standing outside in the wind. "He's the one who looks after the ranch when I'm working on the newspaper."

Nessa was relieved by the interruption. She was having trouble concentrating on today's lessons because she kept thinking about Albert's letter. Also, there were other distractions. Her feet hurt from her tight shoes, and even though she was thrilled to have Ivy back in class, she wished they could sneak away for a quiet talk.

"Why, thank you, Mr. Button. We were just getting ready for recess." Nessa smiled at the noisy procession to the door.

They followed the men across the creek. Hoss was

taller than Mr. Button with a full head of hair that stuck out like fur on a dog. His face was friendly with faint lines creased around his mouth. When he smiled at the children his eyes lit up. Like his older cousin, he wore suspenders to hold up his pants over a full stomach, and his shirt was stained from past meals. He whistled cheerfully.

Two mules were waiting in the field, hitched to a plow. They lifted their heads and brayed in response to Hoss's whistle.

"Here's what," Hoss said to the students. "I'll drive Bess and Betty and you young'uns follow behind far enough so as they don't kick you by accident. Pick up all the big stones you can and carry 'em to the edge of the field. Add 'em to the rocks you put there last time. Makes a nice bumpy border and it'll be easier planting come spring, you'll see. Hee-up!" he called to his animals.

The plowing took much of the warm afternoon. Nessa could feel a pleasant change in the air, a hint of autumn. She was glad to hold class outside in the sunshine and fresh breeze. It made her happy to see the children chasing one another through the grass and to hear their laughter. Green raced between their legs, then barked at them to chase her, too. In her excitement she ran into the creek, around a willow, then back again. Three times she made this figure eight, running as fast as she could. The uproar from the children calling her name and trying to catch her made Nessa laugh and want to join in.

Before dismissing her students for the day, Nessa stood with them on the garden's knoll, looking out over the prairie.

How she loved being outside in the wind. She pointed to the northern sky where a flock of Canada geese could be seen flying in a straggled *V*. From high up the birds honked to one another. Ring-necked pheasants rose from the brush to take flight.

Along the riverbank, leaves were clustered in golden piles as the wind swirled them from branches to the earth. She knelt down to show Sven and the others tiny paw prints in the mud, made by raccoons that had come in the night to drink. Augusta and Lucy correctly named the tracks of turtles, deer, and rabbits marking the sandy beach. They all stood quietly to observe a small, black-headed woodpecker drill its beak into an overhead branch.

Were it not for the mosquitoes, Nessa could have lingered until sundown.

When Nessa carried the scraps from dinner out to the pig, she noticed Rolly in the corral with Wildwing, brushing him.

"Nessa," he called to her. "Can you help me check his foot?"

Rolly held the colt's head and spoke soothingly to him while Nessa knelt in the dirt as Mr. Bell had shown them.

Carefully, she lifted the hoof. "It looks about the same," she said, "but I think we could probably file this part that's grown again. What d'you think?"

They exchanged places so Rolly could look. Wildwing stood patiently, as if he were a big horse that knew this was important business.

"Yes," said Rolly. "I think so, too. I'll be right back."

He returned from the barn with the file.

"I hope I don't hurt him," he said. "Here, boy, this'll just take a second."

When he was done, Rolly looked up at Nessa with a smile. His yellow hair was mussed and windblown as usual.

"Nessa, I think someday you'll be able to ride Wildwing, and we can go out together. When you're high up on a horse, you won't believe how pretty the prairie is. You can see forever."

CHAPTER FIFTEEN

Loaves and Fish

In September, the soldiers' chaplain left Fort Larned for another post. And Reverend Ames returned to his congregation in Independence, because his tenure as Prairie River's minister had come to an end. The townspeople would have to wait for another reverend to fill the rotating position.

In the meantime, church was still held at the schoolhouse. Some of the men in town took turns preparing sermons and selecting hymns for worship. The folks of Prairie River hoped one day to have a piano or organ to fill the small room with music. But until then they would continue to sing from their hymnals.

Just a few weeks later, Nessa was in Mr. Filmore's store buying coffee beans. Mr. Button was there, discussing with several men their hopes for a new preacher. Apparently, a letter had just arrived from a minister in Missouri, a colleague of Reverend Ames who wanted to come west. When Nessa heard the name McDuff, she felt dizzy.

Hurrying home with the coffee, her heart beat fast.

This couldn't be happening. If he showed up, the town was so small it would be impossible to avoid seeing him, and she wouldn't know what to say if he approached her.

She found Mrs. Lockett in the yard, unpinning laundry from the line. Nessa leaned against one of the posts to catch her breath. She looked out at the windswept prairie and the wisps of clouds high above. Flocks of ducks rose in the sky, their green wings glistening in the sunlight. The Indian boy and his friends were out there somewhere, a thought that still made her uneasy.

But Nessa was more upset by what she had heard in the store. "Mrs. Lockett?" she asked. "If Reverend McDuff shows up here, will you give him room and board like you did for Reverend Ames and the others?"

The sun was at Mrs. Lockett's back, casting a halo around her golden hair. Wind snapped the sheets and blew them around their legs as Nessa reached out to fold them into a hamper.

"Honey," she said, taking a clothespin from her mouth, "if puttin' up this gentleman would make you squirm then, no, I won't do it. I'll tell him to lodge with the Applewoods or at one of the ranches."

Nessa looked at the woman's clear blue eyes and smiled. "Thank you, Mrs. Lockett."

Mr. Filmore, Ivy's father, stood in front of the small gathering, smiling self-consciously. It was his first time delivering the sermon.

Looking around, Nessa was pleased that on Friday her students had helped polish the windows and sweep the schoolhouse floor. They had moved the desks against the walls to make room for benches and chairs that were brought by wagon each Sunday by various families. She looked around, exchanging waves with Mr. and Mrs. Bell. All her students were there with their younger siblings, most of whom fidgeted in their seats. A few women held babies. Ivy was between Mrs. Lockett and Minnie. Two soldiers in their crisp blue uniforms sat with their wives. Their voluminous hoopskirts took up so much space no one else could share their bench.

Fanny Jo and Laura were in the front row next to the Applewoods. Nessa wished the sisters would turn around so she could see if they were still angry with her. She wasn't sure how to go about being friendly again, knowing how badly she had disappointed them.

"Good morning, everyone," said Mr. Filmore. His white shirt looked freshly starched and was fastened at the neck with a black string tie. His vest was unlike any Nessa had ever seen. It was made from pieces of brown and white and blue calico, patched together like a quilt. She wondered if Ivy had made it for him. He held his Bible in his left hand and began flipping through the Book of John, wetting his finger with the tip of his tongue, to better turn the pages. As he read about Jesus, his voice gained strength.

"This story begins with a little boy," said Mr. Filmore. "One day this little boy was in a crowd of people listening to Jesus teach. It was hot and windy because it was by the Sea of Galilee. Folks were thirsty. They were hungry, but there was no place to buy food. When Jesus asked His disciples to figure out how to feed everyone, this boy offered to share his own lunch. It was just two small fish the size of sardines and five small barley loaves. Not much a-tall. Jesus didn't laugh at the boy or tell him to run along home. No, Jesus took the small lunch, thanked God for it, and then by a wonderful miracle the food began multiplying. Jesus passed fish and loaves around to all those people sitting in the grass. There were at least five thousand, probably many, many more if you count all the dogs and little boys that follow crowds, mothers, and sisters. Anyway, they ate until they couldn't eat anymore. There was so much bread left over, Jesus told His disciples to gather up all the pieces so nothing would be wasted. And don't you know, they filled up twelve baskets afterward."

Here Mr. Filmore reached into his vest pocket to check his watch. The silver lid clicked when he shut it. He spoke another ten minutes then set his Bible down. "All's I want to say here is that Jesus will give us what we need with plenty left over to share with others. Miracles happen when we're not looking for 'em and they happen for regular everyday things without us even asking. Let's praise God."

He nodded to Hoss, who had come forward to sit on a stool with his guitar. The suspenders holding up his pants were bright blue. Nessa would not have guessed he played the guitar and was surprised he had such a beautiful voice. To her, Hoss sounded like an angel singing. The congregation joined in.

All hail the pow'r of Jesus' name! Let angels prostrate fall;
Bring forth the royal diadem, and crown Him Lord of all,
Bring forth the royal diadem, and crown Him Lord of all. . . .

O that, with yonder sacred throng, we at His feet may fall;
We'll join the everlasting song, and crown Him Lord of all,
We'll join the everlasting song, and crown Him Lord of all.

After supper, Nessa enjoyed her time with Mrs. Lockett, helping with dishes and sweeping the kitchen. Minnie and Rolly had finished their chores and were in the parlor playing checkers.

"I was wondering about something," Nessa said as she began hanging up teacups in the cupboard. It had become easier for her to express herself, because Mrs. Lockett didn't interrupt her and often waited before giving a thoughtful response. Nessa trusted her.

"Yes, dear?"

"Remember what Mr. Filmore said this morning about the loaves and fish, and about miracles?"

"I've been thinkin' on it all day m'self."

"Well," said Nessa, "when Mr. Filmore sings, he praises God with such a strong voice, he's so hopeful . . . I just wonder . . . I mean, where was a miracle for him when Ivy's mama and sisters were dying? Didn't he feel that Jesus let him down?"

"Hmm . . . well, let me ponder it a bit." Mrs. Lockett carried the dishpan to the back porch and dumped the water in the bushes. When she returned, she hung the pan on the wall, took off her apron, and led Nessa outside. They stood in the yard listening to the wind flap the wet dish towels on the line. In the west, the sun had left behind a pale blue glow from its setting two hours earlier. The eastern sky was a deeper blue, with flickers of stars. From the bottomland came the *hoo-hoo* of an owl beginning its night hunt.

Mrs. Lockett rubbed her arms for warmth. "Nessa, I reckon this is what Mr. Filmore's talkin' about," she finally said. "Every day that we wake up and breathe is a miracle from God. We can count on the sun risin' and the sun settin'. Even when the clouds hide the sky we know God hasn't taken away the moon and stars and sun. The birds sing every morning — I ain't heard one day in my life when they didn't. Now it's autumn. Grass and leaves are dyin', geese are findin' their winter homes, soon snow'll come. Just as surely as the cold winds'll blow across this prairie, God will bring spring again with warm air and newborn baby animals."

She looked at Nessa. "My dear, I ain't never talked to Mr. Filmore about his loss, but I reckon he's thankful for the everyday miracles that we don't ask for, but we need 'em to live, and we need 'em to keep goin' another day. It's how I can keep praisin' God, even though my Charlie ain't come back from the war yet, and we don't know if he ever will."

Nessa felt the wind through her dress as they stood under the darkening sky. On the dirt by their feet was a rectangle of yellow light from the open kitchen door. As she considered Mrs. Lockett's words, she looked inside and noticed Rolly sneaking out of the pantry with a handful of cookies. Nessa smiled. A hopeful thought occurred to her.

She would again try to write a letter to her aunt and ask about the twins. If they were still alive, they would be ten years old and they, too, might be sneaking sweets from someone's pantry.

Nessa wanted to find the rest of her family.

CHAPTER SIXTEEN

―――≫◆≪―――

Ivy

When Ivy didn't come to school Monday, Nessa wondered if she'd made another mistake and somehow had offended her again. She felt distracted all morning. Then at recess, she looked toward Filmore's store in town. She noticed a group of soldiers marching toward the cemetery. Two coffins in the back of a wagon were draped with an American flag.

Rolly came up beside her. "Mr. Button said there's some sort of epidemic at the fort."

Nessa looked at him. "Really?"

He nodded.

Nessa had a hard time concentrating all day. After dismissing her students that afternoon, she rushed to Mr. Filmore's store. Nessa was surprised when a clerk from the seamstress shop greeted her. Nessa couldn't remember a time that Mr. Filmore had not tended the store himself.

"They're to home," the clerk told her. "Miss Ivy ailin' bad."

Nessa flew outside and hurried past a corral to the

small sod house. She knocked on the door, her heart in her throat.

When Mr. Filmore opened it, his appearance was much changed from yesterday in church. His hair was askew and his eyes were swollen, as if he hadn't slept all night.

With a motion of his arm, he ushered Nessa inside. "Before supper yesterday she had a headache and fever something awful," he said. "She couldn't eat anything. I thought the worst — cholera — but the surgeon came at midnight and said it wasn't."

A curtain hanging from a beam in the low ceiling separated the room. Ivy's bed was in a corner. Yesterday after church, Ivy's brown hair had glistened in the sunlight as she and Nessa walked home. She had chattered happily about wanting to plan a picnic for Rolly and Howard. But now Ivy lay on a pillow soaked with sweat, her braids tangled by her neck. Her eyes were closed. A rash of pink spots covered her cheeks and damp forehead.

Nessa turned to Mr. Filmore. She was afraid to say anything, but after a moment she took courage. "Is it smallpox?" she asked.

"No, thank God, no," he said. "The surgeon says it's more 'n' likely typhoid, but . . ." He rubbed his forehead, then ran his fingers through his beard.

Nessa caught her breath. Her eyes pleaded with Mr. Filmore. "Typhoid? Will Ivy . . . ?"

With a heavy sigh, he lowered himself into a chair and shook his head. "I don't know, sweetheart, I don't know what'll happen. These past hours I've been praying for a miracle. She's all I got left."

Panic raced in Nessa's heart. She feared for this man who had lost nearly everything, but had come to Prairie River to begin a new life. She feared for Ivy, and she feared for herself.

At long last, Nessa was making a friend. Would Ivy be taken away from her now, after they'd made amends and were starting anew? Would Mr. Filmore be left without any family at all?

She fell to her knees at Ivy's bedside and took the girl's hot hand. Nessa pressed it to her cheek, feeling the fever through Ivy's fingers. She remembered how thrilled she had been when Ivy forgave her and now she wanted to do something in return. Nessa wanted a chance to be a true friend.

"*Dear Jesus,*" she prayed aloud, "*You multiplied the fish and loaves, You give us everything we need and then extra. Please, Lord, we're asking for a miracle for Ivy. We need her . . . please don't take her away.*"

A muffled sound came from the chair. Nessa turned to see Ivy's father with his face in his hands. Hearing him weep brought immediate tears to Nessa. She choked them back, her heart aching for him.

"*Oh, Lord, show me what to do,*" she whispered. "*Show me how to help.*"

Ivy stirred. Nessa gently removed her wet pillow and replaced it with a rolled-up towel.

"Is this better, Ivy?" she asked. "I'm going to change

your bed so you'll have nice clean sheets. You'll feel so much better, I promise."

Mr. Filmore was quiet now. With tired eyes, he watched Nessa move about the room. She started a fire in the small iron stove and put some water in a pot, ladled from a bucket by the door. Quickly, she tidied the room by putting dirty spoons and bowls in a dishpan and sweeping the floor.

"Mr. Filmore," she said. "I'll be right back to sit with Ivy, then you can rest."

Nessa hurried home. Mrs. Lockett was preparing supper, but she showed Nessa where to find a clean sheet and pillowcase. Minnie helped pack a basket for Mr. Filmore. In it were slices of crisply fried turnip, an apple, and a sandwich thick with ham and beef. Meanwhile, Nessa ran upstairs.

Nessa knew that in her trunk was a folded nightgown and other personal items that must have belonged to her mother. When she opened the lid, the pleasant smell of rosemary and lavender greeted her.

Carefully, she looked through the layers of clothing. She found the embroidered nightgown packed between petticoats. She pulled it out and held it up to the window where the afternoon light shone in at an angle.

It was a beautiful gown, white with yellow lace woven into the neckline. The sleeves were loose with buttons at the wrists. Nessa held it to herself, breathed in its good smell, then folded it and brought it downstairs.

━◆◆◆━

On the path from the boardinghouse, Green trotted alongside Nessa, her ears alert as if she knew what lay ahead. When they arrived, Mr. Filmore had pulled his chair beside Ivy and was stroking her hand.

Nessa changed the bedding, and while Mr. Filmore stepped out to the privy, she bathed Ivy with a warm cloth from water heated on the stove. She brushed Ivy's hair into one long braid.

In her fevered state, Ivy didn't recognize Nessa. "Mama?" she cried in a hoarse voice.

There was a lump in Nessa's throat as she dressed Ivy in the clean nightgown. Somewhere deep inside her was a memory that she, too, had called out for a mother who was no longer there. A sudden anguish touched Nessa, but she was not going to let herself cry. The last thing she wanted to do was upset Mr. Filmore more.

After Nessa smoothed the covers, Green jumped onto the bed and lay her yellow head across Ivy's feet.

Next, Nessa set the sandwich on the table and poured Mr. Filmore a cup of hot coffee. She wondered if either of them might catch Ivy's sickness while caring for her, but didn't want to ask the question aloud.

"Mrs. Lockett made up your supper," she told him. "We'll bring you breakfast, too, come morning."

He folded his hands over his plate then bowed his head.

"*Dear Lord,*" he said, his voice breaking. "*Thank You for my good neighbors and bless them for their kindness. I give You thanks for this food and . . . Lord . . . please hold my daughter close to You. . . .*"

Mr. Filmore fell asleep with his head on the table. Nessa washed the dishes and opened a window for fresh air. She sat by Ivy. At midnight, a clock on the shelf chimed twelve times. The next thing Nessa heard was the chirping of birds. Sunlight streamed in through an open door and there was an aroma of bacon frying.

"'Morning," said Mr. Filmore. He cracked six eggs — one by one — into a skillet sputtering with butter. "You'll need breakfast before heading off to school, sweetheart. I'm most grateful to you for watching over Ivy last night. I checked on her. She's still fevered, but I'll take over from here."

After eating, Nessa sat on the edge of Ivy's bed. "I've got to go now, Ivy, but I'll be back. I can't wait until you're better and can return to class."

Nessa squeezed the warm hand but got no response.

CHAPTER SEVENTEEN

———◆———

A Friend Loves at All Times

Each day after school, Nessa bathed Ivy with a sponge and brushed her hair, talking to her as if they were having tea together on a regular day. Ivy was pale and her cheeks looked hollow. The rash had faded, but there were still tiny pink splotches. Even though she looked better, Ivy still did not seem to know where she was or who was in the room. Her continual cries for her mother were wrenching to both her father and Nessa.

The surgeon came late one afternoon when Nessa and Minnie were cooking supper for Mr. Filmore. "The reason why folks die from typhoid is because of dehydration from diarrhea," he said. "Sometimes they last a week with the sickness, sometimes two. No one really knows what causes the illness or how to stop it.

"Sir," he said to Ivy's father, "every single hour give your daughter a tablespoon of water, whether she likes it or not. Then pray to God it stays inside of her. It's all we can do. That and keep her dry, her bedding clean. I'll send one of the laundresses over here each morning to collect soiled linens."

The next afternoon another soldier was buried in the small cemetery outside of town.

Nessa's head hurt from worrying.

With each passing day that Ivy didn't get better, Nessa spent more time pleading with God. She prayed on her knees before going to bed, she prayed silently in the kitchen while she washed dishes. She prayed during school as the children studied and while they were outside during recess. She prayed on the way to the store, then again on the way home.

When Peter died she had blamed herself for not having prayed enough for the little boy.

Nessa was not going to make the same mistake with Ivy.

As she worked at the butter churn, Nessa thought of Ivy. The churn was made from an earthenware crock with a broom handle poked through a hole in its lid. Attached to this handle at the bottom was a whisk that stirred the cream. Nessa sat on the back porch with this crock at her knees, churning with all her might, her braid flapping over her shoulder. It was late afternoon, and the sun slanted across her lap. Her arms were tired, but she liked the pounding and swishing sounds.

Mrs. Lockett came up the steps carrying a bundle of clean white dish towels that had been drying on the line. "What's troubling you, dear?" she asked. "I ain't seen you work with so much vigor."

Nessa dropped her hands to her lap and sighed. "I want to do something for Ivy, but she barely knows I'm in the room with her. What if her fever makes her forget that we made up and are still friends?"

Mrs. Lockett spread the cloths along the railing to fold them. "All's I know, honey, is to have a friend you gotta be a friend. Proverbs seventeen says, "A friend loves at all times." I reckon that even though Ivy's not able to chat with you or go to school, there is a way you can let her know you care."

"How?"

"Well, dear, I don't know. That's something you can figure out yourself."

That evening after supper, Nessa looked through her trunk. Carefully, she took out letters bundled with blue ribbon, then looked through layers of clothes. She paused at the thin leather folder that held her mother's drawings. She decided she would return later to linger over the pictures of the house on the lake. Nessa lifted the box with Buddy's collar. As she did, she could hear its tiny bell ring. Under her father's Bible was a cookbook, a stack of magazines, several dime novels, and a pamphlet of poems by Walt Whitman.

One book caught her eye.

Two Years Before the Mast by Richard Henry Dana. This seemed familiar to her. She read the inscription on the inside page.

With love to Claire Christine. This true story is an accurate rendering of our crew's days at sea. Your adoring husband, Howard. 14 February 1855

Nessa read it again. A note from her father to her mother. She wondered if this was the reason she'd heard stories about ships and the ocean, because her father had been a sailor.

In an instant, Nessa knew this was what she wanted to do for Ivy. She would read to her.

Even if Ivy didn't recognize Nessa's voice, maybe hearing a story would make her feel better.

Downstairs in the parlor, Rolly and Nessa played checkers.

"Mr. Bell showed me something today," he told her, sliding forward one of his black pieces.

"What is it?" Nessa double jumped him, capturing two of his checkers.

"Well," he said, "we need to prepare Wildwing to have horseshoes nailed into the bottom of his hooves — it'll be someday, I don't know when — so meanwhile, every time we clean his hooves we need to tap on them gently with the file so he'll get used to it. That way, he won't kick Mr. Bell when he shoes 'im. Now you have to crown me." Rolly jumped three of her reds, landing in her back row.

At that moment, Mrs. Lockett came into the room to blow out the oil lamps. "Time to turn in," she said.

"Mother, you're just in time," said Rolly. "I think Nessa was letting me win again."

In the flickering lamplight, Mrs. Lockett winked at Nessa.

CHAPTER EIGHTEEN

Fog

Fog blanketed the prairie. Nessa looked out her bedroom windows and saw only gray. There was no corral, no fort, no river. Though she had never been on a ship at sea, she had heard stories and now imagined she was on the ocean, peering into a mist. She opened her window and was surprised at the damp air and the quiet. The birds seemed far away. Even the bugle playing reveille was muffled.

Nessa went downstairs and set the table for breakfast. Mrs. Lockett was turning hotcakes onto golden brown stacks that were warming at the back of the stove. Sausage sizzled in her large black skillet.

"Last night, I saw Hoss and Mr. Button at the store," she said, "so I invited 'em to eat with us this mornin', otherwise it'd just be the four of us. The folks who boarded here yesterday left, decided to camp yonder, away from Fort Larned. Scared of typhoid, they said, even though this house ain't got the sickness. We'll manage anyhow, the Lord has always provided."

Nessa knew Mrs. Lockett was referring to lost income. Without guests to pay for meals and lodging, the family had no way of earning money for supplies. And with Mr. Lockett still missing from the war, his soldier's pay had stopped.

"Oh, Mrs. Lockett, don't worry," she said. "I get nine dollars a month from teaching, so we'll make do just fine."

The woman looked at Nessa over her shoulder as she rolled the sausages in their grease. "My dear, what a lovely thing to say. We'll wait and see what happens, and keep prayin' for the typhoid to leave Prairie River, and we'll keep prayin' that God heals our friend Ivy, and that our poor soldiers will get well, too. My word," she said, "those big cousins are standin' on our doorstep, lookee there. I didn't see 'em walkin' through the fog. Do come in, Mr. Button. Come in, Hoss."

Nessa poured the men a third cup of coffee, then set the pot on the stove. It was Saturday, and they were enjoying not having to hurry.

". . . And so I'm gonna be needing some help with the paper," Mr. Button was saying. "I'm pretty busy clearing fields on the ranch but truth is"— he held up his large hands —"setting type is for little fingers. Headlines are easy because the letters are big, but to fit more stories on a page, I have to use the smallest letters, and it just takes me too much time. You gals would be good at it because your hands are dainty, but you're both plenty busy already. So starting today I'll be running an ad, looking for someone."

After Hoss and Mr. Button left, Nessa helped clean the kitchen. Then she called Green and they stepped into the fog. She wore her shawl to protect herself against the damp air. It was strange not being able to see town. The only way she knew which way to go was to keep her eyes on the path in front of her. Soon enough, an adobe wall appeared in the mist, then a warehouse, then the tailor's shop.

At the newspaper office, Nessa gave Mr. Button ten cents.

"Two copies, please."

"Nonsense, young lady. You don't have to pay me."

"But I want to, Mr. Button. You work hard at what you do."

"All right, then," he said. "But let me give your dog a little treat. I saved it from supper last night. Here, Green." Mr. Button reached into his pocket and pulled out his handkerchief. Wrapped inside were two pieces of ham and a chunk of corn bread. He leaned over as far as his big stomach would allow and set the food on the floor. "Here you go, girl."

Green approached the snack, sniffing. With one gulp, the ham and corn bread disappeared. Then she sat on her haunches, her tail stirring dust from the floor. When she raised her paw, Mr. Button shook it as if they were friends meeting on the street.

"How 'bout that," he said. "You've got better manners than most folks I know. Come back soon, Green, you're welcome anytime."

The fog and its chilly dampness made Nessa yearn to be inside. She hurried home with her newspapers because there were three letters she wanted to write before taking her turn to look after Ivy. It didn't take long to find Mr. Button's ad.

WANTED — AT THIS OFFICE, SOMEONE TO LEARN
THE PRINTING BUSINESS. EDITOR WILL SUPPLY
APPROPRIATE TRAINING. SMALL HANDS NEEDED FOR
TYPESETTING. ROOM AND BOARD PROVIDED.

Her first letter was to Albert. She circled the ad in pencil, then folded the paper into an envelope addressed with his name.

Dear Albert,
    I know you're happy with your apprenticeship, but here's an opportunity if you change your mind. The editor, Mr. Button, is a good man and Prairie River is the most beautiful place I've ever seen. If you come, I'll share Green with you. And Rolly — you will like Rolly — he and I'll also share Wildwing.
Fond regards,
Nessa

Nessa's second letter was to her aunt, something she'd been thinking about writing for weeks. She closed her eyes and tried to imagine what she might look like.

Maybe they resembled each other! How Nessa yearned to find her true family. This time she didn't write angry thoughts or crumple up the paper. Instead, she politely introduced herself, inquired after her aunt's health, then asked about the twins.

. . . and someday soon I would like to see you again,
Aunt Britta.
Cordially, your niece,
Vanessa Ann Clemens

P.S. Do you remember my raccoon, Buddy?

Her third letter was to Miss Eva, with one dollar enclosed toward her debt.

Miss Eva,
   I'm so worried for Ivy. She has suffered much in her life and is suffering now. But I'm praying as you taught me and am reading to her from one of my mother's books. Thank you again, Miss Eva, for rescuing my trunk and sending it here.

Nessa took her letters to Mr. Filmore's, where an afternoon stage would be coming from Fort Dodge on its way east. It might be weeks before her mail arrived in Missouri, and probably longer for up north. Racine, Wisconsin, was the address on a letter Aunt Britta had written to her mother twelve years earlier. Nessa hoped she still lived there.

Postage came to one dollar and twenty-five cents. While Mr. Filmore stamped the envelopes, Nessa went to the little sod house to check on Ivy. She also brought along a pan of fresh johnnycake that Mrs. Lockett had baked for the family.

Laura was at the girl's bedside, bathing her face with a warm cloth. Nessa was glad to see Laura, but since her terrible mistake Nessa felt shy about talking to her. In the two weeks since Ivy had become ill, various women at the fort had been taking turns caring for her. Nessa went every day after school, then again after supper, each time reading to her, Green curled up on the bed at Ivy's side.

"She's still sleeping," said Laura. "I'll be here for the afternoon. The surgeon told Fanny Jo to stay away on account of the baby, just in case. But so far I haven't gotten sick from Ivy, neither has anyone else." Laura was cordial to Nessa, but she didn't smile or look her in the eye.

Nessa wanted to apologize again, but remembered some advice Mrs. Lockett had shared with her.

Honey, Mrs. Lockett had said, *some folks don't say if they forgive you or not, they just go on to the next day and the next, and that's what you gotta do, too. Over time, things have a way of smoothin' out. But then again, some folks never forgive. They just stay sour and mad the rest of their lives.*

As Nessa waited for water to boil for tea, she thought about Mrs. Lockett's words and decided to be patient. She set the table with two china cups, then sliced the johnnycake, arranging it nicely on a plate. Laura helped her carry the table to Ivy's bedside. They sat near the sick girl, conversing with her as if she were sitting up with them in a chair.

Laura held Ivy's head and tipped a spoonful of water into her mouth. Some dribbled down her chin, but Ivy was able to swallow a bit, even though she appeared to be sleeping.

"Ivy dear," said Laura, "when you are rosy and well, we're going to have a lovely party for you with cakes and tea and plum tarts. Fanny Jo will be there, and we'll invite Mrs. Lockett and Minnie. You remember Mrs. Bell, don't you? And her little baby, Oliver? He's already five months old. They'll be so happy to see you. . . ."

Laura drew Ivy's blanket up to her shoulders, then kissed her forehead.

A silence hung in the air. Nessa suddenly felt uncomfortable and wanted to run from the room, but instead sat quietly holding her teacup.

It was what Laura *hadn't* said that crushed her. Everyone would be invited to the party except Nessa.

CHAPTER NINETEEN

---◆---

Saturday Supper

By two o'clock in the afternoon the fog had lifted. Nessa hung her shawl on the hook in her bedroom and opened her windows. Once again, the late September sun was as hot as a summer afternoon. When she saw the familiar wagon coming from along the creek she ran downstairs.

"Mr. and Mrs. Bell are coming," she called to Minnie. "The baby, too."

The blacksmith and his wife had been invited for Saturday supper. Minnie ran out the door, followed by Nessa and Green. They loved it when company came, real company. Minnie called them "special guests."

"Mama's boarders stay a few days, then leave," she once explained to Nessa. "But friends, they always come back."

The wagon pulled into the yard with a rattling of harness. Mr. Bell jumped down and handed the reins to Rolly, then came to the other side to help his wife.

"Hello, Nessa," said Mrs. Bell, handing her a bundle of baby. "How are you, dear? And my word, Minnie, did you lose another tooth?"

As Minnie demonstrated how her tongue could poke through the spaces between her top and bottom teeth, she accidentally spit on Mrs. Bell's sleeve. Minnie immediately pressed her hand to her mouth, such was her embarrassment.

"Oh, never mind about that," the woman said. "Oliver drips on me all the time." She smiled kindly at the six-year-old girl. Mrs. Bell's hair was braided in coils atop her head. Her gingham dress had pearl buttons from her throat down to her waist.

Nessa was fond of Mrs. Bell, because she was cheerful and looked for the good in any matter. She and Mrs. Lockett were the only two people in Prairie River who had defended Nessa to the school committee when she had first arrived. And her affection for Mrs. Bell had grown the afternoon when Oliver was born. Nessa, Fanny Jo, and Laura had helped deliver her baby during a thunderstorm. Mrs. Bell had been so strong, yet had reached out to the girls for their support. Peter had been there, too, keeping a fire going in the stove.

Nessa had never seen a baby being born and certainly not on the floor of a schoolhouse. But at last, the storm had ended, and Oliver came into the world with his mother and three "aunties" and a curious little boy gazing at him.

Rolly unhitched the Bells' horse and led it into the corral. Wildwing came over to see the buckskin mare, then lifted his nose to touch hers.

Mr. Bell was wearing a clean blue shirt with black suspenders. He shook hands with Rolly. "How're you doing, son? Let's have a look at your colt."

He stroked its gray back. "Easy, now, you're a handsome fellow, yes, you are." Mr. Bell knelt to examine Wildwing's hoof, then stood up and patted his flank. "Well," he said, "you two are doing a fine job keeping his feet clean and the sore one trimmed. Someday we'll be able to fit him with a shoe that might help him even more. They're straightening you up right," the blacksmith said, giving Wildwing a solid pat.

Mr. Bell turned toward the yard where earlier a soldier had delivered a wagonload of fallen timber gathered along the river. "Want to lend me a hand?" he asked Rolly. "I'd like to help your mother cut some firewood. She'll be needing it sooner than we think."

"Still no boarders, Vivian?" asked Mrs. Bell. The two women were in the kitchen paring apples to bake in a cobbler. Nessa was at the table rolling out dough for its crust. The room had a rich aroma of roast beef and potatoes.

"No boarders," said Mrs. Lockett. "Not since Tuesday."

"My word," said Mrs. Bell. "That explains those folks camped on the other side of the trail, by the river. Lord, I hope everyone heals up quick from the typhoid, and it'll be gone for good."

Mrs. Lockett leaned down to pick up baby Oliver from her clean floor, where he had been on his stomach trying to crawl. "Here's my darlin' boy," Mrs. Lockett cooed to him, lifting him into the air. "Such a sweetheart, up you go!" He had plump pink cheeks and brown hair like his mother's. His face broke into a toothless smile. Below his long shirt were plump little legs and bare feet.

To Mrs. Bell she answered, "I hope so, too, that the typhoid leaves, for everyone's sake. Meantime, we'll just make do. Won't we, Nessa dear?"

Nessa simply smiled and nodded in response.

CHAPTER TWENTY

A Sack of Carrots

Sunday after church, Nessa found Rolly in the corral, petting his old horse, Buttercup. Meanwhile, Wildwing was nuzzling Rolly's pocket where he had hidden a small apple.

"Want to walk Wildwing with me?" he asked her. "The sooner he gets used to you leadin' him around, the better."

"Yes!" she said. "I'll get the rope."

Rolly tied it to the colt's halter and led him out the gate, his slingshot tucked into his suspenders. Wildwing tossed his head and playfully reared up a few times, but Rolly spoke gently to him and continued walking toward the river, Green in the lead. The puppy kept looking back to make sure everyone was following, which seemed to put a prance into Wildwing's step.

"Here, you try," Rolly said after a while, handing the rope to Nessa. "Don't worry about him being wild, Nessa, he's just feeling his oats because he's been penned up." They followed the creek by the schoolhouse, then took the path to Mr. Button's ranch, commenting on how much straighter Wildwing's step was as they made their way.

The October sun was warm. Meadowlarks dipped and soared over the reddish prairie. For miles in every direction the grasses swished in the wind, rolling like a great moving sea. Nessa breathed in the aroma of baked soil and thought it was another perfect day. Overhead, a triangle of geese passed with noisy honking, a marvel that made her smile. She loved these birds and how they always seemed to know where they were going.

Hoss was pitching hay into the back of a wagon when he saw the small procession approach the ranch.

"Say there!" he called, waving them over. "Got something for your horse." He leaned into the wagon and lifted out a burlap sack. From it, he pulled out a stub of a carrot.

Wildwing's ears perked up, and he eagerly followed Nessa over to Hoss, who held the carrot in his open palm. With its soft lips, the colt gummed the carrot, then crunched it into his mouth. At the sound of eating, Green sat politely in front of Hoss and lifted one paw.

"Well, I'll be." He laughed out loud, then bent down to take Green's paw in his large hand. "How d'y do?" He gave her a carrot, his face still creased with a smile.

To Nessa he said, "This sack is for you, saved it special so you'd have a little extra. Me and my cousin are still enjoying those pumpkins you gave us from your garden." He removed his hat to fan his sweating neck, squinting into the sun. His shirt was stained under the arms.

"Here's what," he continued. "An Indian told us it's

gonna be a hard winter, so we better get ready. These carrots should last you a while unless this dog of yours gets
into 'em." He laughed again.

"Thank you so much, Hoss, I really mean it." But at
the mention of Indians, Nessa had started thinking
about the boy and his horse.

"Have you seen many around?" she asked. "I mean,
Indians?"

"Sure have. From the corner of our land we see their
wigwams yonder, by the river. And Button's writing a
story 'bout how the government's gettin' ready to sign a
treaty so we'll be seeing more and more of 'em."

"More?" asked Rolly. Wind blew his yellow hair
around his face. His cheeks were red and chapped from
the sun. He stood a head taller than Nessa. She could tell
he had grown since her arrival in Prairie River.

"Yessir," said Hoss. "They'll be comin' to the fort real
regular to collect the stuff we're gonna promise to give
'em in the treaty. Food, blankets, and what-not." He
looked out across his ranch to where Mr. Button was re-
pairing a fence. Clouds were piled like cotton in the blue
sky.

"Yup," he said. "We'll be seein' Indians, plenty more."

CHAPTER TWENTY-ONE

The Thief

One morning at breakfast, Mrs. Lockett sat down at the table with a sigh.

"I didn't realize we're out of salt," she said to Nessa. "When you're done eatin', honey, would you please go to town and pick some up for me? Mr. Filmore's been out of spices since last week, so you'll need to go to Applewoods'. A two-pound sack'll do. Me and Minnie'll take care of these dishes."

Nessa dipped her spoon in her oatmeal to stir the melting butter and brown sugar. Facing the Applewoods was the last thing she wanted to do on such a beautiful fall day. She'd rather read to Ivy. But she didn't want to disappoint Mrs. Lockett.

"Yes," Nessa answered, "of course I'll go."

She stepped outside into warm sunshine, barefoot. Green trotted ahead of her, for the puppy loved going to town. The wind was no longer hot like summer, but felt cool as it blew through Nessa's sleeves. The sky was dotted with ducks and geese flying in wedges, southward. From the grass came the noisy chatter of black-tailed prairie dogs popping up from their holes and dashing down another.

A girl about ten years old played on the sidewalk of Officers' Row, rolling a hoop with a stick. She wore a frilly dress with a thick blue bow tied at her waist. Nessa guessed her family was new to Fort Larned because she hadn't seen her before. In the dirt nearby, three young boys sat in a circle, flicking marbles back and forth. They, too, must be newcomers.

I should visit their families, thought Nessa, *and invite them to school.*

"Hello, Teacher!" came a tiny voice. "Hello, Green!"

Nessa looked up to see Poppy standing in her doorway. Her pumpkin-colored curls bounced as she waved her hand. Through the window framed with lace curtains Nessa could see the Negro maid, who had answered the door the first time Nessa had been there. She was serving breakfast to Lieutenant Sullivan and his wife.

Nessa waved back to Poppy. She felt so cheered by the friendly greeting, she was smiling when she entered the store. A small bell jingled against the door.

Mrs. Applewood was stringing together clusters of garlic cloves. Hanging from a beam overhead were colorful strands of red chili peppers, onions, cranberries, and slices of dried apple.

"What is it this time?" the woman asked. She reached up to hang the string of garlic on a nail.

Before Nessa had a chance to ask for salt, Mrs. Applewood cleared her throat. "It seems," she said, "that your Mrs. Lockett has run up quite a bill lately."

Two ladies in the store were watching Nessa. Mr. Applewood looked up from a crate he was unpacking and also stared. Nessa felt her face turn red. With everyone eyeing her, she wished she had proper shoes on her feet and that her sleeves weren't so short on her arms.

"Yes, I know," she said. Nessa couldn't believe she was telling a lie and how easy it was to do so. "I've come to settle the account. If you would kindly give me the total, I'll be right back to pay you."

Without looking in her ledger Mrs. Applewood said, "Thirteen dollars and twenty-five cents." She must have memorized the amount and kept it ready in her head.

"Thank you, Mrs. Apple —" Nessa stopped herself with a cough. She had almost said Apple*worm*, a mistake she didn't want to make today. She turned for the door and hurried home, Green running alongside her.

Nessa was relieved to see Mrs. Lockett busy in the barn. Without being noticed, Nessa slipped in the kitchen door and ran upstairs. In her trunk, inside her mother's hatbox, was the purse she had carried with her from Independence. Miss Eva had sewn it from one of her handkerchiefs. It was there that Nessa kept her money.

She spilled the bills and coins onto her bed to see how much was there, then scooped it back into her purse.

Quickly, before Mrs. Lockett might come into the house and wonder why Nessa had returned without the salt, she tucked the handkerchief into her sleeve and rushed back to the store with Green.

As Nessa counted out the coins, the storekeeper eyed her suspiciously. "So, if no boarders have been stoppin' at your place, how is it Mrs. Lockett suddenly has money? I asked her three times already for payment. Does she have cash buried in the yard?"

Nessa swallowed hard. She glanced at Mrs. Applewood's tight bun on top of her head. How she wanted to grab it and mess up her hair. She wanted to shout, *None of your business, you old so-and-so.*

Instead, she concentrated on counting. ". . . eleven . . . twelve . . . thirteen dollars" — now came pennies and nickels — ". . . twenty-three, twenty-four, twenty-five cents. There you go, Mrs. Applewood. And here's another eighty cents for the salt." Nessa's new pair of shoes would have to wait.

The woman immediately went into the back room to put away her money.

When Nessa set the bag of salt on the kitchen table, Minnie burst into laughter. Rolly pointed to Green.

"When did your dog start playin' poker?" he asked.

Nessa turned around. Green was coming up the back steps with something in her mouth. It was a thin white box with red lettering on the side.

"Oh, no," she said. "I have a bad feeling about this. Green, drop it right now."

Green sat, but would not open her mouth.

"Drop it," Nessa said again.

Green's eyebrows moved as she looked first at Minnie, then Rolly. She would not look at Nessa.

Finally, Nessa kneeled and pried open her puppy's jaws. Out came a soggy pack of playing cards. "Where did you get these, you naughty girl?"

Then she remembered Mr. Applewood had been stocking shelves when they came into the store. He must have turned his back long enough for Green to look inside one of the crates and take the first thing she found.

"Now what?" Nessa wondered aloud. She slumped against the table, the wet cards in her hand.

"I know," said Minnie. "Just go to the Applewoods and say Green took 'em."

Nessa laughed, but shook her head. "Oh, they'll never believe *that* story, even though it's true. Ever since I arrived in Prairie River, they've been hinting that I'm a thief, waiting for this day — to catch me stealing — or so they'd like to think."

Rolly said, "Well, at least give 'em the twenty-five cents. I saw their sign, that's what playing cards cost. Me and Minnie'll go with you, Nessa. I ain't afraid of those folks."

Nessa remembered counting out her last pennies upstairs on her bed. She had ten cents left. She didn't want to draw attention to the fact that she'd spent all her wages because it might embarrass Mrs. Lockett. The cards couldn't be returned because they now had teeth marks in them and would be warped by the time they dried out.

She looked across the kitchen floor where Green had made herself comfortable against the wall. She was lying on her back, paws in the air. It seemed she hadn't a care in the world.

Mrs. Lockett bit her lip to keep from laughing. "What're you gonna do, honey?"

"I don't know," Nessa answered. "Reckon I got to think on it somewhat."

"Well, anyhow," said Rolly, bending down to pet Green's belly, "you got the trickiest, sneakiest, bestest dog I ever did see."

CHAPTER TWENTY-TWO

The Old Mountain Man

The next day when Mrs. Lockett asked Nessa to buy a sewing needle, Nessa still hadn't figured out what to say to Mrs. Applewood. So instead, she went to Filmore's.

The store was busier than usual, with soldiers and townsfolk making purchases and exchanging news. When an officer began describing an Indian attack, Nessa listened carefully.

". . . killed three of our men, alls they were doin' was sleepin' peaceful-like by the campfire, rolled up in their saddle blankets . . ." The man was small in stature, but sturdy. Markings on his coat indicated he was a colonel with the New Mexico volunteers. His hair was the color of sand and was greased back off his forehead, hanging below his ears. A thin mustache covered his lip. He was animated while telling his story, using his hands to describe events.

". . . then from my belt I drew a single-barrel pistol. The shot missed 'im but cut the string holding his tomahawk, then . . ."

Nessa thought this was some of the most dreadful

news she'd ever heard. She nervously fingered the lace on her sleeve.

The story continued with gruesome details. Nessa guessed this officer was a traveler spending the night at Fort Larned because she hadn't seen him before. The soldiers in the store listened to him with rapt attention, giving him the respect of an elder. Only when he mentioned California, did she realize he was describing another place and time.

Nessa was relieved, but now wondered if the same thing could happen here at Pawnee Creek.

"So, about those men there," said the colonel. He pointed out the window to the parade ground, where a company of soldiers was marching.

Mr. Filmore offered him a plug of tobacco. "This is on the house," he said, then poured him a glass of whiskey. "Those boys out there are the Second U.S. Infantry, we call 'em 'Galvanized Yanks.'"

"Heard tell about those boys. War prisoners, ain't they?"

"That's right," said Mr. Filmore. "Johnny Rebs captured by the Union. They were let out of the stockade if they volunteered to come west, so here they are."

The officer leaned forward to spit into a bucket by the counter. "Well, sir," the man said with a laugh. "Nothing like some fresh air and three squares to help a fella change his opinion on political matters, ain't that so?"

The soldiers laughed in agreement. Nessa gathered that Mr. Filmore and the officer were describing life at the fort compared to life in a jail. It seemed that some prisoners cared more that they weren't hungry than on which side they had fought. She noticed Rolly, Big Howard, and Sven had slipped into the store and had become part of the observant crowd. Sven and Rolly looked as if they could be brothers with their wild yellow hair and sunburned cheeks.

Nessa stepped forward to the counter and purchased the sewing needle, which Mr. Filmore wove into a small piece of canvas so it wouldn't prick her. But she was so fascinated by the colonel's stories she couldn't bring herself to leave the store.

For the next hour she listened to him tell about fur trappers, grizzly bears, and fights with Indians. He mentioned encounters with many different tribes. Nessa marveled at the exotic names — Comanche, Navajo, Cheyenne, Klamath, Utahs, Sioux, Modoc. Then he rubbed his left shoulder, where he'd been shot by a Blackfoot warrior. It had been in the dead of winter, near the Big Snake River.

"Would've bled to death," he said, "but the night was so bitter cold, the wound froze solid and stuck to my shirt, makin' the blood stop. I lived to see the sunrise, thanks to Providence." He put the whiskey glass to his lips and tilted his head back for one long swallow. Then he settled his hat on his head.

"Good visitin' with you folks." And the man went out the door toward the parade ground, a slight limp to his walk.

When the door closed behind him, the crowd that had gathered erupted in loud discussion, retelling the officer's stories with further detail.

"Mr. Filmore?" asked Nessa. "Who was that soldier?"

He gazed out the window. "Why, probably the most famous mountain man that ever lived, that's who. Colonel Kit Carson," he said. "Knows so many languages and customs of the Indians that the government asked him to be part of the treaty business, near here at the Arkansas River. He was one of the peace commissioners. No finer man, in my opinion."

At supper, Rolly couldn't stop talking about Kit Carson.

"A real Indian fighter," he said, spooning mashed potatoes onto his plate in the shape of a mountain.

Nessa passed him the pitcher of gravy. "I think he's more a peacemaker now," she said. "Don't you think he looked tired? There were dark circles under his eyes."

"Nope." Rolly cast a dreamy look at the ceiling. "I wish he woulda let us see his scars."

Three gentlemen at the table had also been in the store during the colonel's visit. They smiled at Rolly recounting the stories to his mother and sister.

Mrs. Lockett poured the men coffee to go with their cobbler, then sat down with a basket of mending. Nessa noticed she was sewing a piece of scarlet cloth, scarlet like she had seen in Mrs. Applewood's store.

CHAPTER TWENTY-THREE

An Anonymous Donor

Nessa woke in the middle of the night, shivering. Wind groaned through the eaves. Sleet hissed at her windows. As she sat up to unfold her buffalo robe and pull it over herself, someone knocked on her door.

"Yes?"

Mrs. Lockett peeked in, her arm around Minnie. "Honey," she whispered, "do you mind if Minnie shares your bed? We got several travelers frozen to the bone that just arrived on the late stage. There's a lady, too, so I'm givin' her Minnie's bed with the curtain pulled around it to make a little privacy. I'm puttin' Rolly in the parlor. Goodness knows their room is even tinier than this one dear, but we need the —"

"Of course," said Nessa. "Come here, Minnie, wait till you see how warm this old buffalo is." She tucked the sleepy girl in against the wall and patted the foot of the bed for Green to jump up.

"Mrs. Lockett, do you need any help?"

The woman's braid fell over her shoulder as she bent down to kiss Minnie. "Well," she said, "if you don't mind — I want to get those folks warmed up with some hot coffee. The cobbler you baked for supper, Nessa, would do nicely and there's still some fresh . . ."

Without needing further explanation, Nessa stepped out of bed onto the cold floor and wrapped her shawl around her nightgown. Over this she wore her apron, put on a pair of woolen stockings, then followed Mrs. Lockett downstairs.

Three days later the gentleman and lady left to resume their journey to Los Angeles. They would be escorted partway by some of Fort Larned's cavalry, then their trail would split onto a southern route for California. Mrs. Lockett accepted their coins, then put them in her small leather purse. This she hid in the pantry, deep in the flour barrel.

She dusted off her hands, smiling at Nessa. "I knew our good Lord would provide. He's rarely early, but He ain't never been late."

Nessa was relieved that once again boarders were coming to stay. But it was November and the weather was turning cold. Soon traffic on the Santa Fe Trail would dwindle, and travelers would become even more scarce.

Later that afternoon, a Catholic priest and his assistant arrived on their way to the pueblo of Taos. After Nessa made up their beds and served them some stew, Mrs. Lockett went into the pantry.

To Nessa she whispered, "I'll be right back, honey. Finally, I got somethin' to pay the Applewoods for my account."

Nessa opened her mouth to speak, but said nothing. She hadn't thought about this moment, but now remembered that sooner or later Mrs. Lockett would come to learn she had paid the bill for her. Nessa would be embarrassed when the woman returned with appreciative remarks, but she would try to be gracious.

For the next hour Nessa busied herself by cleaning the parlor with the feather duster. Bookcases framed the stone fireplace where the priest sat reading. She dusted these shelves, the windowsills and furniture, the ceiling corners, then the stairs. By the time Mrs. Lockett returned she had dusted the entire house.

Through the railings in the stairway, Nessa watched Mrs. Lockett hang up her cloak and bonnet, then start upstairs. She was carrying a brown parcel tied with string.

When Mrs. Lockett saw Nessa sitting on the top step, she stopped to give her a tender look.

"There you are, darlin'," she said. "Such good news of an afternoon, what Mrs. Applewood told me. Plumb brought me to tears, it did. Nessa, it seems someone paid our entire bill, thirteen dollars and twenty-five cents. When I asked Mrs. Applewood who, she said the person insisted on bein' anonymous. I am completely flabbergasted."

Nessa, too, was flabbergasted. "Really?" she said.

Mrs. Lockett continued upstairs to her room to put away her purchase. "Quite an honorable person to pay a stranger's debt without broadcasting his deed. Whoever he is, I'm askin' the Lord to bless his kindness."

Nessa was too startled for words. Her mind raced with conflicting thoughts. Why did the storekeeper spin a story that only she and Nessa knew wasn't true?

Then Nessa was filled with guilt. Had she paid the Lockett's bill only to be praised? Or had she truly done so out of love, wanting to help the family that had been so generous to her?

And was this God's punishment because she herself had lied to Mrs. Applewood? Now more than ever Nessa was sorry she hadn't been truthful, though at the time she had only meant to spare Mrs. Lockett embarrassment.

Lord Jesus, I'm confused and frustrated all over again!

Nessa slumped on her bed, looking out the window. Her room was cold. Gray clouds covered the sun. A hawk circled high in the wind, then dove suddenly toward the earth. Hidden for a moment, it then took flight, its fringed wings pumping the air. A small animal dangled from its beak.

Nessa wished she were that hawk and could fly away for a few hours. She felt sour toward Mrs. Applewood and yet ashamed that she felt so.

In Nessa's quiet moments she had begun reading her father's Bible. Now she took it out of the trunk and leaned against the wall, her buffalo robe over her knees. Already she felt comforted by the warmth of the fur and by holding in her lap something that had been important to her father.

She turned the pages, not knowing what she was looking for. She'd never seen a Bible where its owner had underlined and circled passages, and written notes in the margins. There was a story here about her father's life, but so far it was a mystery to her.

Her eyes fell on a verse in Proverbs 15. It wasn't marked, but it caught her attention just the same.

The eyes of the Lord are in every place, beholding the evil and the good.

Nessa considered this. Whether Mrs. Lockett ever learned the truth about who paid the bill, it didn't matter. God knew. And she herself knew, and her deed had made her feel good.

From where Nessa sat she could see only the wind-blown clouds as she looked out the window. She liked to pray this way, imagining God was in the sky watching everything and smiling down on her.

Lord, please help me forgive Mrs. Applewood — again! I don't like her much at all, even though You love her. I'm sorry about that, and I'm sorry about telling a lie. Please help me be gentle and accepting.

Nessa's eyes felt heavy, but she blinked hard to wake up and forced herself to get out from under her warm robe. It was Saturday. She wanted to read to Ivy. Even though her friend was still too ill to recognize her, Nessa wanted to finish reading chapter five of their book, about the tiny ship *Pilgrim* sailing around the treacherous Cape Horn.

CHAPTER TWENTY-FOUR

A Perfect Fit

It was late October. A raw wind scoured the prairie. Snow flurries whitened the sky, but were blown away before being able to blanket the cold ground. Mrs. Lockett's kitchen was warm and glowed with lantern light. After supper, while three guests lingered over coffee, Nessa hurried with Minnie to wash the dishes and sweep the floor. She wanted to spend the evening in her room.

Spread out on her bed were the letters from her trunk and some of her mother's artwork. She remembered as a small child seeing her in a window seat with a sketchpad on her lap, the sun coming in over the penciled drawings.

It made Nessa feel good to see pictures of their house by the lake, all from her mother's hand. She guessed the portraits were of friends and forgotten family members. There were simple scenes, too: a child's wagon . . . apples lined up along a porch railing . . . a canoe. Her favorite was of her pet raccoon, Buddy, his tiny front paws holding a strawberry. This reminded Nessa of her letter to Aunt Britta and how eagerly she hoped for a response.

Nessa heard a rattling of paper from the other side of

her door. She got up and looked into the hallway. On the floor was a package wrapped in newspaper, tied with string. Nessa's name was written on top.

"Hello?" she called out. But no one answered.

Puzzled, she took it into her room, sat on her trunk, and untied the string. The newsprint fell away, revealing a folded garment of soft cotton. The color was scarlet.

Nessa caught her breath when she realized it was a new dress. She held it up and tried to see herself in her mirror, but the reflection was too small, just the size of a dinner plate.

"Mrs. Lockett!" she cried, running downstairs. She found her in the kitchen, grinding coffee beans. Nessa danced in front of her with the dress pressed to her. "I love it. . . . Oh, Mrs. Lockett, thank you."

The plump woman smiled. "I thought that color would look pretty on you, honey, and my, does it. I've been wantin' to sew you a new one since the first day I saw you. Gonna try it on?"

"Oh, yes!" The clamor of Nessa running upstairs sounded like three girls.

She stepped into the dress and pulled it up over her chemise. Tiny black buttons rose from her waist to her neck. Black piping framed the collar, which cupped her chin. Her sleeves fit nicely and buttoned at her wrists with black lace. The skirt was a perfect length, just touching the tops of her toes. It was the most beautiful thing Nessa had ever worn. And the color. How she loved this deep red.

Flooded with gratitude, she ran her hands over the smooth material. Tears stung her eyes. How could she ever thank this kind woman?

Nessa brushed her hair into one braid and experimented with coiling it at the nape of her neck. But the pins kept falling to the floor, and after twenty minutes she gave up. Maybe next spring when she turned fifteen, Mrs. Lockett could teach her how to twist her hair atop her head like Laura and Fanny Jo. Then she would look like a real lady.

Nessa still avoided Mrs. Applewood. Now it was because she didn't think she could look her in the eye without feeling embarrassed. They both knew the truth, but neither was saying. So when Mrs. Lockett asked Nessa to buy a box of candles, once again she went to Filmore's instead.

Minnie was with her when they stepped in the store out of the wind. The girl brushed her fingers over Nessa's new dress.

"It's so soft," she said, "and pretty. Does it twirl?"

"Watch," said Nessa. She spread her arms inside her shawl and did a twirl, her eyes closed. It felt so good, she did another. It was wonderful to finally have a dress long enough to hide her old shoes.

As she spun around she felt herself bump into someone. When she opened her eyes, her heart thumped in her chest.

It was the Indian boy. He stared at her as he had that day in the cemetery. He didn't smile.

"Pardon me!" she cried, backing up. The boy wore a blue-and-white-checkered shirt with a deerskin vest. His trousers were denim and his moccasins came up to his knees. Behind him stood an older Indian, a man with white braids. A dark-haired woman wrapped in a blanket was beside him.

"Nessa," said Mr. Filmore, "this old man is Chief Poor Bear, from the Apache. He and these folks are here to pick up supplies and speak with the Indian agent. I'm not sure what tribe the boy's from, but an interpreter is supposed to be here in a few minutes."

Nessa was too surprised to speak, but she managed to nod with respect. She had been so busy showing off to Minnie, she hadn't noticed the visitors in a corner looking at the shelves of food. Despite her embarrassment, she was surprised to not feel afraid. All these weeks she had dreaded running into this boy, but suddenly she had done just that. It also was some relief that he didn't smell like a skunk this time.

She wondered if he liked wearing a shirt buttoned up to his chin. He seemed uncomfortable in these fancy clothes.

"Hello," she said to the visitors, but they didn't return her smile.

CHAPTER TWENTY-FIVE

Good News

It was still dark outside when Nessa woke to voices coming from the kitchen, earlier and louder than usual. She wrapped her shawl around her shoulders and crept downstairs. The floor felt cool to her feet this morning. She had decided to stop wearing her shoes until she could buy a pair that would fit her better.

As she came down the stairs, she saw Laura by the stove. A lantern hanging from a rafter cast shadows under her eyes. Her braid was wispy, as if she hadn't yet combed her hair, but she was smiling.

"Oh, there you are!" she said, when Nessa came into the light. "I'm so happy you're up. Quickly, come see Ivy. Her fever broke an hour ago, and she's sitting up in bed. I just came looking for another clean blanket and to borrow this tub from Mrs. Lockett. Ivy asked for a bath, that's how awake she is."

Nessa was so relieved by this wonderful news, she let out a whoop as she ran upstairs to get dressed. God had answered their prayers!

Mr. Filmore's house was warm with lamplight and a fire in the stove. Laura poured boiling water into the tub, stirring it with cooler water to make a perfect temperature.

Nessa had brought her long, white apron, which she now tied over her dress so it would stay dry. She thought she might need help getting Ivy into the bath, but her friend was so light and frail, Nessa felt as if she were lifting a doll. Green curled up on the rug to watch, her chin resting on her paw.

"My, oh, my," said Ivy as she sank into the steamy water, her eyes closed. "This is . . . so nice."

Mr. Filmore had gone to the store to give the girls privacy. Tenderly, Laura and Nessa washed Ivy's thin arms. They unbraided her hair and poured warm water over her head, massaging her scalp with lavender soap and oil scented with mint. The tub filled with suds.

"Oh, Ivy, I missed you so much," said Nessa. "We were worried, so worried, but I prayed every day that the Lord would bring you back to us, and now here you are. Even Green worried about you and slept at your feet. See, here she is now."

Ivy opened her eyes and smiled. She lifted a sudsy hand to pet Green's head, then laughed at the bubbles on the yellow fur.

"Hello, Green," she said in a hoarse voice. "Now I remember. You were a good nurse. . . . You made me feel warm when I was cold." Ivy's lips were dry and cracked. Her cheeks were hollow, but her eyes sparkled.

They wrapped Ivy in the clean blanket and settled her in front of the stove so her hair could dry. They fed her warm broth with bits of chicken and potatoes then changed the bedding. Together, Laura and Nessa hauled the tub of water outside to dump in the grass.

By the time they returned to the cabin, the sun was rising in the eastern sky and Ivy was asleep.

"I'll stay, Nessa, so you can get to school on time." Laura said this while gathering soiled linens into a basket. She glanced at Nessa with a smile.

"Thank you," said Nessa. She leaned over the bed to whisper. "Ivy, I'll be back before supper."

As Nessa turned to leave the cabin, she stood for a moment with her hand on the door latch. She looked at Laura, hoping for another sign of friendliness, but Laura was busy hanging the wet towel over a chair.

CHAPTER TWENTY-SIX

A Cloud in the Distance

When Nessa arrived at the schoolhouse, she was still wearing her apron. She started to untie the bow, but then thought it might be a good idea to keep it on, so her new dress would stay clean. As she approached her desk, she was surprised to see Big Howard arranging a gray wool blanket on the floor by her chair. He looked up at his teacher.

"Green needs a place to sleep," he said. "Soon the floor'll be cold. Here, girl." He patted the soft bed until Green came to investigate.

"There you go," he said, scratching behind her ears and under her chin. "Even brought you a treat." From his shirt pocket, Howard scooped out some popcorn and fed Green, piece by piece. He gave Sven a handful so the new boy could also make friends with Green.

Seeing her puppy curled on the soft bed, Nessa smiled at the boys. "Howard," she said, "it was kind of you to bring Green a blanket and such a nice treat. I really appreciate it, and I'm sure Green does, too." She turned to face the class.

"Hello, everyone. It's a lovely morning and —"

But she realized Augusta and Lucy weren't listening to her. They were whispering. Even when Nessa opened her Bible to start reading, the girls didn't stop.

To get their attention, Nessa cleared her throat.

Augusta pointed out the window. Her brown pigtails stuck out above her shoulders.

"Yes? What is it, Augusta?"

"A storm's coming."

Nessa turned to look. The sky was blue except for a low gray cloud in the east. Wind streaked it sideways.

"We'll be all right, girls. The storm's a long way off and may not even come this far. Besides, Mr. Button and Hoss built a good wooden roof so we'll stay dry if it rains." Nessa was remembering the thunderstorm last summer when Mrs. Bell's baby was born right here in the corner by the stove. "Don't worry, we'll be safe."

"Let's begin class. I would like to start with *John eight, verse twelve*," she began reading. Miss Eva had her memorize these words of Jesus when she was five, and she wanted her own students to learn them as well. "*. . . I am the light of the world: he that followeth me shall not walk in darkness, but shall have the light of life.*"

Nessa then dictated from Proverbs 2, so they could practice penmanship. "*Verse six: For the Lord giveth wisdom: out of His mouth cometh knowledge and understanding.*"

This took nearly fifteen minutes, for the children wrote slowly.

Minnie raised her hand.

"Yes, Minnie?"

"I'm done, Miss Nessa, and I'm thirsty, but the bucket's empty. Can I go to the creek to fetch more?"

"Good idea," said Nessa. "Be swift now. We begin arithmetic soon."

Minnie ran out the door with the pail. While the others were carefully spelling the last word — *understanding* — Nessa cleared her throat again. The children had resumed whispering. This time, Sven raised his hand.

"Yes, Sven?"

He had a husky voice for an eight-year-old. "Miss Vanessa, I smell something."

Nessa lifted her head.

Smoke.

She got up from her desk and walked to the window. The cloud they had seen earlier was building, now filling the sky.

Rolly came to stand next to her. He whispered to Nessa, "It ain't a storm."

Then Nessa noticed what he had seen. The bottom of the cloud glowed red.

Fire.

"Children," she said, trying to keep her voice calm. "We're going home early today. We'll go together, so everyone stay by me. You may grab your dinner pails on the way out."

"But what about my sister?" Rolly asked.

Nessa hurried to the other window to look for Minnie, but didn't see her on the path.

"Don't worry, Rolly," she said. "We'll take the road along the creek and find Minnie on the way."

As she led her students out the door, a roar of wind filled the air with dense smoke. It stung her eyes and choked her. Nessa could no longer see the tall flag flying from Fort Larned. In order to reach town they would have to run through the cloud. Already she and the children were coughing and wiping their eyes.

"Let's go," she called above the wind. Her dress and long apron whipped around her legs. When she turned her head, her braid flipped across her face, prickling her cheeks. With growing alarm, Nessa realized the fire might pass between the fort and schoolhouse, blocking their way home.

Meanwhile, the children were calling the puppy. "Come back!" cried Lucy. "Miss Vanessa, Green's running away."

Nessa had momentarily forgotten Green, but she must take care of her students first. Through her stinging eyes she regarded each child. They were all there, except Minnie. Nessa was too frightened to pray, though in her mind she was crying out to God.

An idea came to her. "Howard," she called. "Run inside and get the blanket, please. . . . Quickly now, run! We're going directly down to the river instead of taking the road."

Nessa lifted Poppy to her hip to carry her for she was having trouble keeping up. Lucy and Augusta clung to her skirt. The boys followed closely behind. Howard had caught up to them, the blanket gathered in his arms.

As they headed for the creek, a sudden assortment of birds flew overhead, soaring wildly in the wind. Rabbits

and ground squirrels bounded in front of them, fleeing
the fire, then a family of raccoons. Prairie chickens ran,
flapping their wings. There was a horrible noise of
screeching animals. Nessa kept turning around to make
sure the children were with her.

"Minnie!" she cried into the wind. "Minnie, where are
you?" The children called Minnie's name, too, and
Green's.

Nessa's heart was in her throat. Everything was happening so fast! If only she hadn't let Minnie leave the
classroom. And where was her puppy?

At the riverbank, the smoke seemed to lift. *Perhaps we
will be safe here,* Nessa thought. But at that moment,
Rolly grabbed her shoulder.

"The wind's shifting," he yelled. "Look."

The tall grasses were now blowing toward them.
Smoke hid the schoolhouse and the road to town. It was
indeed blocking their way home. Nessa was stunned.
They were trapped. Their little sod school was probably
burning, and there was no place to go except into the
water itself.

"Follow me!" she cried. Nessa led her students down
the sandy bank into the stream. The girls' dresses floated
up to their waists. The water was so cold, she soon felt
chilled and knew they couldn't stay here long. Nessa also
worried the current would sweep them off their feet. She
held Poppy tight because the girl was so small.

The sky was black. A great howling wind covered
them with smoke. The fire was coming this way, from the
direction of the schoolhouse. She could smell burning

grass and hear it crackling. Nessa's heart beat wildly as she fought the panic rising inside. She must be brave for she was their teacher and they were depending on her. When she saw the confusion on their faces yet how they stayed by her side — trusting her — her mind raced with thoughts and worries all mixed up. *What are Mr. Applewood and the others thinking?* she wondered, but then realized their opinion wasn't important now.

The shortest of prayers escaped her lips: "*Jesus!*"

What should they do? If they stayed in the water, the fire might pass over them, but their wet clothes would be heavy and could pull them under. The youngest children might drown.

Another thought terrified her. What if Minnie had tried to find the schoolhouse, but got lost along the way? Mrs. Lockett would be shattered, they all would be. How would Nessa ever be able to live with herself?

After five minutes of struggling to stay together in the strong current, Nessa changed her mind and led everyone back to shore, to sit on the beach. She hugged Poppy, at the same time reaching for the other children to reassure them. Sven patted Lucy's hand because she was crying.

Then through a break in the wind, they heard a dog barking.

CHAPTER TWENTY-SEVEN

Green

Nessa peered through the smoke, looking in every direction. There was no mistaking her puppy's bark, but where was she? A shift in wind momentarily lifted the black cloud so they were able to see across the creek to the patch of dirt that had been their garden.

"There she is!" shouted Howard.

The children cried her name, but the dog wouldn't come. She was barking frantically, running back and forth between the creek and garden.

Nessa realized Green had found a place without smoke.

"Howard and Rolly," she yelled, "dunk this blanket all the way underwater till it's soaked through, but hurry!"

It was hard to walk in her wet dress because it was heavy and chafed her skin, but she led the children along the bank to the footbridge they had used all summer. It was actually a series of wide stones from which to leap, but soon they were all across, their lunch pails abandoned behind them.

"Children, run!" Nessa cried.

Twice Green raced from the garden to the creek, all the while barking and circling them as if herding a flock.

When they reached the dirt, Green jumped on Nessa, knocking her down.

"Good girl!" she said, grabbing the fur around her neck and hugging her. Nessa looked around her. Sven stood with Rolly and Howard, who held the dripping blanket. Augusta and Lucy had Poppy between them, holding her hand.

They were all there. Except Minnie.

Nessa took a deep breath, coughing from the smoke. Her lungs hurt. Quickly, she decided she must return to the creek, leaving Rolly in charge. The garden was smaller than an acre, but if they stayed in its center they'd be safe. Surely fire wouldn't burn this soft dirt, if it even came this far. The river would be a natural barrier.

"Rolly," she shouted. "I'm going back to find your sister. Everyone stay here. . . . Get down as close together as you can." Nessa threw the blanket over the huddled children and ran.

She was not going to leave Minnie behind.

Dense smoke rolled across the grass. Green bolted ahead of Nessa, stopping now and then to sniff the air and listen. She thought she heard the sound of a mewing kitten come through the wind. It was high-pitched and frantic. It was a long moment before Nessa recognized Minnie's voice.

"Minnie," she cried, "I'm coming! Where are you?"

Another cry. Nessa pulled her dripping dress above

her knees and ran to the river. She looked down over the embankment and saw Green below her, crouched in the mud, tail wagging. The puppy was staring inside an overhang of roots.

Nessa slid down the bank. Minnie had crawled under a stump of a willow that formed a small cave. Water was up to her shoulders. Her lips were blue, her face sickly pale.

"Oh, Minnie," said Nessa. She reached for the girl, who was too numb to move, and pulled her onto shore. "Oh, Minnie, you were so smart to hide here. Now let's go join the others. . . . Rolly's waiting for you. Can you hurry?"

Minnie nodded, but her shivering was such that she couldn't stand.

Nessa's heart sank. Her dress was too sopped to run, and Minnie too heavy to carry. She held the girl close to her. *Should we wait here?* she wondered. *But what if the children panic and flee?*

A crackling sound drew her attention upstream. Flames had jumped the river and ignited saplings on the other side. Now the only way to avoid the fire was to swim. But Nessa knew their bulky dresses would pull them under.

With no time to think or pray or cry, Nessa untied her soggy apron and threw it to the ground. Then she drew her full skirt up to her waist, scooping Minnie as if in a sling. Clenching the cloth in her fists, Nessa stepped and leaped across boulders to the other side, one hundred yards from the new fire. To her relief, she saw the children still huddled under the blanket. Flames licked along the embankments, but had not yet moved up the slope to the garden.

With all her strength, Nessa ran to the dirt, cradling Minnie inside her dress.

CHAPTER TWENTY-EIGHT

Under the Blanket

"As close together as you can!" Nessa cried to the children as she crawled under the blanket with Minnie, pulling Green into their midst.

Lucy was crying.

"It's all right, honey," Nessa told her. "We're just hiding from the fire. Soon it'll be gone."

The blanket was heavy with water and oozed onto their necks. It stunk of wet wool. Nessa lifted an edge to peek out. Orange and red flames burned with terrible speed up the slope from the creek toward them.

The children began praying in a jumble of heartfelt cries.

"Lord, please keep the fire away. . . ."

"I'm scared. . . ."

"Protect us, please, Jesus —"

Nessa interrupted them. "Hold the blanket tight," she yelled. "Hold it down so it doesn't blow away."

A blast of heat rolled over them with a *whoosh*. Gusts of wind pulled at the blanket and filled their little tent with hot, steamy air.

Nessa clung to Green's collar, afraid to look out. Poppy was curled next to her, trembling like a small bird. Wind pushed at them from every direction.

It seemed forever, but finally Nessa lifted her corner of the blanket.

The fire was on the far side of the garden, moving away. Cautiously, Nessa sat up, then so did the others. Puffs of smoke dotted the scorched landscape. The prairie looked like the stubble of a man's beard.

When she realized they were safe at last, Nessa felt as if she would collapse. Her insides were shaking uncontrollably, from cold and nervousness. She felt sick to her stomach. Her new red dress was caked with mud.

"It's all right, children." She sounded calmer than she felt, her voice hoarse from the smoke. Coughing into her hands, she swallowed a sob, hoping the children didn't know how frightened she'd been.

Nessa stood with her students in the center of the field. It was charred as if heat had singed the bits of dried grass poking out of the plowed dirt. But their blanket didn't seem to have been touched by fire.

"Is everyone all right?" she asked, checking them for burns. Their cheeks were streaked with soot, and their clothes were still wet. Nessa noticed the wind was making them shiver.

"Stomp your feet," she said, "and wave your arms."

When Rolly saw how his sister was shaking from cold, he removed his shirt and drew it down over her shoulders. Though wet, it was warm from the heat of his own body. Howard and Sven did the same with their shirts.

Lucy took Minnie's hands and rubbed them between her own, and Augusta stood behind Minnie to vigorously buff the girl's arms.

"We'll get you warm," said Lucy, "and don't you look pretty wearing the boys' shirts like a shawl, as if you're going to a party."

"Do you like hot rum?" asked Augusta. "That's what my ma drinks when she's cold. Maybe your ma'll give you some."

Rolly playfully tugged at Minnie's dripping pigtails. He opened his mouth to say something to her, but his lip began quivering and instead he turned away.

Nessa looked across the creek to where the schoolhouse stood. The roof was gone and the walls were burned to half their height. Mr. Button's fine wooden ceiling had probably gone up like a torch, taking with it some of the sod bricks. Nessa wondered if their desks were gone, too, but her thoughts turned to Mrs. Lockett and Ivy.

Had the town burned, and the fort, too?

Minnie's voice was weak from crying. "I . . . want . . . my . . . mother. . . ."

"We'll take you home right now," said Nessa, glancing at Howard. He lifted Minnie into his strong arms and headed for town.

CHAPTER TWENTY-NINE

"They're All Here"

𝕸rs. Lockett was the first to reach the bedraggled group. Her hands flew into the air when she saw them.

"Oh, my word!" she cried, before bursting into tears. She lifted the hem of her skirt to run as fast as a plump woman could. "We was sick with worry when we saw the smoke, but by the time we headed this way, fire blocked our path, kept us from gettin' to the school."

She grabbed her daughter and held her close. At this, Minnie began wailing.

"It's all right, darlin'." But Mrs. Lockett couldn't stop her own tears of relief. "My, my, I thought I'd lost all of you. Come 'ere, Rolly — you, too, Nessa." She folded them into her arms, weeping. "Thank You, Lord Jesus."

Lieutenant Sullivan was also there, hoisting Poppy in the air to get a good look at her. Mrs. Sullivan held her handkerchief to her eyes. Townspeople hurried along the road toward them with parents of the other students. Mr. Button's shirt was stained with ink, and he had a pencil behind his ear. Hoss rode up on horseback.

No one asked why the three boys were bare chested or why the children were muddy.

"They're all here," said Hoss after counting out loud and touching each child on the shoulder. "Every one of 'em plus Miss Vanessa. Here's what. We were in town prayin' as if to break our hearts. And here you are, safe and sound. God is good, yes, He is."

In the kitchen, Minnie sat by the stove, her feet in a pan of hot water. As it cooled off, Mrs. Lockett would drain some with a ladle, then add more from the boiling kettle.

"Just sit still, honey," she said. "Since I ain't got any rum, we'll just have to warm you up this way, and with hot soup and tea. I thank God Nessa found you when she did, and Rolly, what gentlemen you and Howard and the new boy were to give your shirts. I am mighty proud of you all. Lord, I wish your papa was here to see how brave his son and daughter . . ." Mrs. Lockett was overcome with emotion. She turned to look out the window at the afternoon sun, wiping her cheeks with a dish towel.

"Pardon me," she said after a moment. "Nessa, I ain't got the words to thank you for what you did today."

Nessa didn't know what to say. Her throat ached with wanting to cry. She was exhausted and grateful.

Thank You, God, she kept saying in her mind. *Thank You.*

Nessa had unbraided Minnie's hair and was brushing out the tangles so it would dry faster. The girl was dozing in her chair. As Nessa looked around the kitchen, her heart swelled with affection. Rolly was chopping walnuts for a cake recipe while Mrs. Lockett spooned molasses into a large bowl. Green watched from under the table, waiting for something to spill.

If it hadn't been for Green's instinct, Nessa may never have set eyes again on this peaceful scene. She marveled how a dog could find a spot with no smoke. And how did a six-year-old girl know to hide in the stream, under the roots of a tree?

What mystified Nessa the most was her prayers. Today they had only been thoughts — quick jumbled ones — not real words, yet God still protected everyone. During Ivy's illness, Nessa had prayed night and day, sometimes hourly, and Ivy's fever had finally left.

If God answered according to how much or how little she prayed, then she and the children would have perished in the fire. Minnie would have drowned.

How does God work? Nessa wondered. *Why do some things end well, but others don't?*

Minnie's hair was almost dry, and she had fallen asleep sitting up. Nessa carried her into the parlor, which was warm with coals in the hearth, and lay her on the sofa, tucking a quilt around her. Two gentlemen sat reading by the window where sunlight spread over their laps. The pipes they were smoking gave off a pleasant scent. The room was quiet. Just the slow tick from a clock on the mantel. Nessa kissed the girl's hand.

"You're so smart, Minnie." Kneeling at her side, Nessa prayed for her.

"And Jesus," she whispered, *"I'm grateful You kept us safe today. Thank You for helping me find Minnie."*

CHAPTER THIRTY

No Job

While Minnie napped in the parlor, Mrs. Lockett took Nessa upstairs. Hanging behind the woman's bedroom door was a faded blue dress that had seen many washings and afternoons drying in the sun. She lifted it from the hook and handed it to Nessa. It smelled of soap and fresh air.

"It's clean, darlin'," she said. "It might be big around the middle on account of my size, but I'm givin' it to you just the same. My mother always said a girl ought to have a pretty dress to make you feel special and a regular one for regular days. Here you go, and here's another apron. Its sash'll make a nice bow and no one'll know the difference. Meantime, we'll wash this wet one you're wearin'. It'll be as good as new. By the by, Mr. Filmore was over earlier sayin' Ivy's been askin' for you and —"

"She has? Really? Oh, thank you, Mrs. Lockett!" Nessa rushed to her room, unbuttoned her muddy dress, and changed into the blue one. The cotton was soft with lace at the wrists and neckline. It felt good against her chafed skin as she ran downstairs and to the sutlers' compound.

Nessa knocked, then opened the door. Ivy was sitting up in bed, her hair cascading over her shoulder. The book in her lap was *Two Years Before the Mast*.

"Oh, Nessa, I was so worried about you," said Ivy. "When we saw the smoke, we were frantic. Papa made me stay here, so all we could do was pray. Are you all right?" Ivy covered her mouth with a handkerchief as a fit of coughing seized her.

By the side of the stove was a bucket of water. Nessa dipped in the ladle and took a drink to Ivy. She was bursting with happiness. Ivy had been reading their book. The fever hadn't made her forget they were friends after all.

As the sun traveled lower in the sky, the days grew steadily cooler. The aroma of wood smoke filled the air. With the arrival of each stagecoach, Nessa hoped for letters from Albert, Miss Eva, or her aunt Britta. Most of all, she hoped there would be news about Minnie and Rolly's father, Captain Lockett.

Every day, Nessa read to Ivy. She sat in a chair next to her bed, her bare feet tucked under the warm feather mattress, the book propped on her knees.

"I think my papa was a sailor like this author, Mr. Dana, was," Nessa told her. "I wonder if he gave up sailing on the open seas when he married my mother."

"He must have been very brave," said Ivy, "and I bet he

loved your mother very much." Her voice was soft, and she often coughed hard, trying to clear her throat. Though her fever was gone, she had yet to step outside into the fresh air and sunshine. She could stand for only a moment before her legs would start shaking and she would need to sit down.

The surgeon had said it could take weeks, maybe months before Ivy would be up and walking around. And she might have a queasy stomach for the rest of her life.

"It's a disease that knocks folks off their feet for a long time," he told Mr. Filmore last week. "That is, if it don't kill 'em first."

Ivy had been asleep during this conversation, and Nessa had been filling the stove with firewood. At the surgeon's words, Nessa had felt her courage fade.

". . . Keep her warm. . . . Don't let her go outdoors. . . . may not survive winter . . ."

Recalling the surgeon's warning, Nessa looked at Ivy. The girl's face was so pale it seemed translucent. Her thin hands rested on the coverlet. The possibility that Ivy might not live through winter made Nessa feel cold and sick inside.

She couldn't bear the thought of being abandoned by her new friend. It almost made her want to stop spending time with her. In her heart, Nessa knew that the more she allowed herself to care for Ivy, the more devastated she would be if she were to die.

Then she considered something the headmaster, Mr. Carey, had said. While trying to convince Nessa that there were several benefits to marrying Reverend McDuff he told her the minister did not want to have children — as if it were a wonderful thing.

Now Mr. Carey's words haunted her: *No children, no heartbreak.*

Nessa didn't want to be like either of those two lonely men. Would she refuse to take Ivy as a friend, just to avoid the pain of losing her?

She reached for Ivy's cool hand and placed it in hers. The girl's eyes fluttered as she struggled to stay awake.

"I'm sorry, Nessa," she whispered. "I'm just so sleepy."

"Don't worry, Ivy. Just rest. We'll read after supper tonight or whenever you're ready." Nessa tucked the quilt around Ivy's thin form and felt her forehead.

Good, she thought, *still no fever.*

Later in the week, the school committee gathered. Nessa was reading to Ivy when Mr. Filmore came in from the meeting.

"Folks can't decide whether to even rebuild the schoolhouse, a-tall," he said. "Applewoods and others want to wait till spring. Said the town'll save money by not having to pay out your salary."

Nessa leaned back in her chair and closed her eyes.

"What's wrong?" asked Ivy as her father stepped outside for firewood.

Nessa wanted to keep her worries to herself. She especially didn't want to trouble Ivy after she'd been so ill.

A moment passed. "Well," said Nessa. Another moment passed. "If there's no school until spring, I'll have to find a way to earn money. Worse, what'll the children do about their lessons? Lucy and Augusta are finally beginning to read, and we were just getting to know Sven."

"Something will work out, Nessa."

Nessa gazed out the window. She knew finding a job might not be easy. She was embarrassed to admit she might have to go back to Missouri. "Ivy, you see, I told myself that if I can't make it here on my own, I'll have to leave —"

"What? You mean leave Prairie River?"

Nessa nodded.

"You can't go, Nessa. You belong here. Maybe my father could pay you to help in the store. He likes you a whole lot." Ivy covered her mouth with a handkerchief to quiet her cough. Her body shook as if with a spasm. Finally, she whispered, "Please don't go, Nessa."

As if to herself, Nessa said, "I wish Albert were here —"

Ivy touched Nessa's hand, hooking her little finger with hers in a show of friendship. "Who's Albert?" she asked. Her face showed concern as if she truly wanted to share Nessa's burden.

Nessa sighed. "Albert is my friend," she said. "We know everything about each other — he's the only one my age I've ever been able to really talk to. Who really cared about me." She glanced up at Ivy. "That is, until now."

Ivy squeezed Nessa's hand.

This time Nessa didn't hide her feelings. Her eyes pooled with sudden tears. "We've known each other since we were four years old. . . . We arrived at the orphanage the same week and were so lonesome for our families. . . . It was hard. . . . When Mr. Carey, the head-master . . ."

Nessa stopped to gather her thoughts. Ivy was watching her with tenderness, one tear wetting her cheek.

"Go on, Nessa," she said. "You can tell me. Keep talk-ing."

And Nessa did.

CHAPTER THIRTY-ONE

———◆———

A Small Idea

After breakfast, Nessa put on her blue dress and brushed her hair into two braids, tied back with a matching blue ribbon. She felt nervous having to again ask for a job. Hoss had told her some laundresses made forty dollars a month, more than many of the soldiers. Washing clothes would be hard work, but at least Nessa could help buy supplies for the boardinghouse.

Barefoot, she walked the long way around the fort to Suds Row.

The next morning, Nessa was sweeping Ivy's front step, feeling cheerful about the day. The laundresses were willing to let her help them for a few hours, to see how she would do. If Nessa worked hard, maybe they would recommend her to an officer's family. Just then, Laura arrived for her turn at sitting with Ivy.

"Hello," said Laura. "I was just next door at Filmore's to pick up some yarn. He asked me to give you this."

Laura handed her a letter.

"Oh, thank you," she said as she leaned the broom

149

against a wall. There was a hopeful leap in Nessa's heart. She didn't recognize the handwriting, so maybe it was from Aunt Britta.

In the upper left corner there were initials with an address.

MJM

SECOND STREET CHURCH

INDEPENDENCE, MISSOURI

A sick feeling rolled inside Nessa. Her throat felt so tight, she could barely speak.

"I have to go now," she whispered.

Nessa stormed back to the boardinghouse, her arms swinging at her side. Her heart raced with anger. *How did he find me?*

In a few minutes, she needed to leave for Suds Row. If she read the letter before leaving, she might be too upset to work properly. If she left it on her bureau until she returned home, she knew she would feel distracted all day. But then if she took it with her, the temptation to read it would be too great. She wasn't sure if she would be strong enough to face anyone afterward.

Lord, what should I do? I don't want to sin, but I want nothing from this minister, even if he is one of Yours. Please show me.

Nessa wished God would just answer her in a resounding voice so she could be sure of what He wanted her to do. She sat quietly on the end of her bed, her eyes closed, waiting. She heard only the wind and the distant rattling of wagons from the trail. There was no voice or message from Heaven. Just a small idea came to her.

Calmly, she went downstairs into the parlor. At Mrs. Lockett's rolltop desk, she uncorked the jug of ink and dipped in a quill. In neat block letters she wrote three words across the top of the envelope: RETURN TO SENDER.

Nessa blew on the ink so it would dry, smiling to herself. She wasn't telling a lie by writing "addressee not here," and she wasn't going to ruin her day by wondering what Reverend McDuff had written. As she walked back upstairs to straighten her room, a peace settled over her. She believed with all her heart that she had done the right thing in coming to Prairie River. Since she did not love the dreary minister, Nessa also believed it wasn't a sin to refuse him. She would not let such doubts plague her anymore.

She flung open her window and breathed in the cool autumn air. Sunlight touched her face. In the distance, three teams of oxen pulling covered wagons were nearing Fort Larned. Their white canvas tops billowed in the wind. A stagecoach passed them, turning for the side road leading into the fort. Nessa knew it would stay overnight to rest its horses then leave tomorrow morning for the East. Carrying mail.

"Such a beautiful day!" Nessa cried out to the chittering sparrows.

On her way to Suds Row she would drop off the letter at Filmore's. Now her mind would be free to ponder other things, such as what to do about those playing cards Green stole.

CHAPTER THIRTY-TWO

He Answers

$\mathcal{N}$essa's hands were gooey with flour from the dough she rolled out on the table. It was her first attempt at making crust, but she wanted to surprise Rolly with a chicken pie for supper. Today was his fifteenth birthday.

Nonetheless, a worry sat on her heart as she worked in the kitchen. It was the fifth day without school since the fire. The laundresses had said she was a good worker, but they didn't need her help after all.

A knock on the front door drew Mrs. Lockett from her dishwashing. She returned a moment later, smiling.

"Someone's here to see you, darlin'," she said.

Nessa rinsed her hands in the dishpan then wiped them dry with her apron. She wished she felt more cheerful.

Rushing from the kitchen, Nessa saw Mr. Applewood standing in the parlor by the bookshelves. At the sight of him, Nessa suddenly remembered the stolen deck of cards. *He must be here to accuse me,* she thought. Her throat felt dry, but she was ready to confess.

"Hello, Mr. Applewood."

"I'll get to the point," he said without looking at her. "The committee decided that instead of waiting till spring, we're going to start rebuilding as soon as possible, before the ground freezes, which could be any day now. The children need a schoolhouse, the town needs a church, and I admit it'd be a long winter without either. Hoss and Mr. Button have a sod cutter we can use. The privy burned down, so we'll need a new one of those, too."

He reached in his vest pocket to take out his spectacles. Hooking the wire rim over one ear then another, he settled them on the end of his nose.

"Something here I gotta read to you." He unfolded a square of paper and held it toward the window's light.

"We hereby do declare that Miss Vanessa Ann Clemens be granted a salary of twelve dollars a month to begin immediately. Fort Larned's library shall be temporary quarters for class. School may resume day after tomorrow."

Mr. Applewood unhooked his glasses and returned them to his pocket with the folded paper.

Nessa wanted to jump and clap her hands. She still had a job and now more pay.

"Oh, thank you, Mr. Applewood," she burst out. "This is wonderful news. Thank you."

He gave her a stern look. "Mind you, it wasn't my idea." He turned for the door. His hand rested on the knob as if he had more to say.

Nessa felt her stomach tense. Right about now he

would say something mean, she just knew it. It always happened.

Over his shoulder, he looked at her. "My nephew, Howard, tells me the children were saved on account of you and that dog."

Then Mr. Applewood was out the door. Through the parlor window, Nessa watched him walk from the porch to the steps. His suspenders looked like two lines down his back as he took the path to town. The road curved toward the creek then disappeared around a knoll.

In the kitchen, Nessa picked up the rolling pin and returned to her piecrust. Mrs. Lockett was at the other end of the long table. She looked up from the flour she was measuring for the gravy. "What is it, dear?"

Nessa repeated what Mr. Applewood had told her. "And a raise, too," she said. "I'm so surprised . . . and grateful." Nessa treasured in her heart that God had anticipated her need, even though she'd forgotten to pray specifically about her job.

"Well, darlin', that's just wonderful. Now we have two things to celebrate tonight." Mrs. Lockett handed her a cast-iron pan, deep enough for a whole chicken cut up. While Nessa arranged the dough for the bottom crust, Mrs. Lockett went to the stove to stir her pot of gravy.

"Here," she said, "pour this over the chicken and potatoes, but not too much. Then pinch the top crust over the rim." Mrs. Lockett watched her prick a hole in the rounded top of her pie, then slide it into the oven. After Nessa closed the heavy iron door, the woman gave her an affectionate pat on her cheek, leaving a dusting of flour.

"If I may say so, dear, you're becomin' one fine cook. Rolly is gonna love your birthday supper. I only wish his pa was here to help us celebrate, to see how his son is growing into a man. Charlie would be mighty proud of both of you. My, my, a real schoolteacher under our own roof."

CHAPTER THIRTY-THREE

Something New

A cool relief spread over the land, and the overnight frost killed summer's mosquitoes. Nessa stood in the yard, breathing deeply of the fresh air. She was eager to go see what was left of the school, if there was anything salvageable for class tomorrow. Until now, she hadn't wanted to look.

"Rolly?" she called into the barn where he was cleaning out the milking stall. "When you're finished, want to go with me? I'm bringing Wildwing."

"Coming!" he said. "I'm almost done. Five minutes, I reckon."

Nessa went to the corral. The dirt felt cold to her feet. She hoped Mr. Applewood would pay her soon, before it snowed, before it would be too icy to walk barefoot. She had seen a pair of ladies' shoes in his store. The price was two dollars and fifty cents, the same as a hoopskirt and the same as a box of clothespins. But all that remained in Nessa's savings were ten pennies. She didn't want to ask Mrs. Lockett for a loan while still owing money to Miss

Eva. And Mr. Applewood was the last person she would want to buy from on credit. She imagined he would lecture and shame her until she repaid him.

She would just wait.

Wildwing tossed his head and trotted over to Nessa with a friendly nicker. She tied the rope to his halter. As she led him through the gate, he lipped at her apron pocket where she had hidden a carrot.

"First let's walk a bit," she told him, stroking his gray neck. She ran her fingers through his mane and lay her cheek on his forehead. Wildwing had the good smell of a horse that has been out in the wind and sunshine. It seemed her and Rolly's colt was growing, for he was now taller than her shoulder. And as Green high-stepped beside them, she realized her puppy was also bigger. Nessa could pet her without bending down. At five months old, Green was almost a grown-up dog.

The prairie looked like a shadow under gray autumn skies. The fire had burned a ragged path around the schoolhouse and across the river, disappearing toward the horizon. A shift in wind had turned the flames away from Mr. Button's ranch just in time.

With no roof over the schoolhouse, the room was bright though the sky was overcast. Wind blew through the hollow places in the walls where windows had been. Everything made of wood was gone: the door and window frames, desks, and floor. Nothing remained of their papers and pencils. Nessa bent down by what had been her chair and saw her Bible. The leather cover was burned away and a section of charred pages lay fluttering in the wind.

She felt sad. This was the only thing from the orphanage that had belonged to her. And how would she read verses to her students each morning now? Her father's Bible was too large to carry back and forth from school.

"I'm sorry your Bible got burned," said Rolly. "It's a real shame. You know, I heard soldiers talking. They said that sometimes Indians start prairie fires to thin out the grass. They say it makes it easier for them to hunt antelope and smaller game. But Hoss thinks this one was from a campfire on the trail. Grass is so dry, wind blowing just one spark would do it. Last year before you came, there were three wildfires, but they didn't touch the fort. I'm glad for that."

Nessa smiled at him. His chatter made her feel better. She gave the schoolhouse remains another long look. "Ready to go, Rolly?" She grabbed Wildwing's rope, then started running through the narrow path of buffalo grass that hadn't burned. She ran with her arms in the air as if she were flying a kite, her colt loping beside her with only a slight limp. Green and Rolly raced to catch up. She felt exhilarated by the cool wind and the air that smelled of cooking fires and wood smoke. Nessa loved autumn.

They arrived at the fort out of breath and laughing because Green had been running circles around them, yipping with excitement. Wildwing pranced as if in a parade. It was nearly time to help Mrs. Lockett prepare supper, but Nessa wasn't ready to go home yet. It was too nice being outside in the fresh air.

"I know," she said to Rolly, "let's visit Ivy and show her how big Wildwing is."

They led the colt to Mr. Filmore's house and tapped on the window. In a moment, Ivy's pale face was behind the glass, smiling.

"Oh, Nessa," she said, opening the window, "he's adorable. May I give him a treat? Hello, Rolly. I'm glad to see you both." A moment later, she reached out with two halves of an apple.

"One's for Green, too, because I know how she likes apples. Nessa, can you come in for a minute? I have a surprise."

Nessa handed Rolly the lead rope and let herself in the door. On the table was a pair of ladies' black high-buttoned shoes. They were new. A silver buttonhook was next to them.

Ivy nodded encouragingly at her friend. "I noticed you need shoes, Nessa. Go ahead, they're yours."

Nessa was astonished. "Really? But why?" When she picked them up and felt the soft leather, she wanted to cry. There was not a scuff or mark on them. She had never before worn new shoes. Part of her worried that she should not accept such a generous gift. What if her friend had paid for them with her own money?

"Ivy, are you sure?"

Ivy laughed, then covered her mouth to cough. She coughed for nearly a minute before recovering her breath, then wiped her lips with her handkerchief. "Yes, I'm sure," she said. "They were Sarah's, my older sister. Mama gave them to her on her birthday, but she never had a chance to wear them. Papa agreed that you should have them."

"Oh, Ivy." Nessa held the shoes to her chest. "They're so elegant. But shouldn't you keep them for yourself?"

"I have Mama's shoes, they're in my trunk," said Ivy. "I'll start wearing them when I'm well enough to go outside. Then you and I can walk to church together. We can walk all over the prairie if we want to. I can't wait. And when you read to me tonight we'll have tea just like Sarah used to make."

Nessa rushed to hug her friend. How good it felt to be forgiven and to be wanted.

Ivy felt fragile in her arms, and started coughing again. Her cough concerned Nessa but now knowing that Ivy was determined to get well, her heart soared. She couldn't wait until they could step out onto the prairie together and spend hours talking as if they were real sisters.

CHAPTER THIRTY-FOUR

The Library

After breakfast, Nessa went upstairs to get ready for school. All night she kept waking up, thinking about her new shoes. It touched her deeply that Ivy gave her something that had belonged to her sister. And that she had noticed Nessa's need.

Lord, thank You for Ivy. Thank You for giving me a true friend.

Now, as she buttoned up her shoes, Nessa was grateful for the hook that was like a short knitting needle. It slipped into each narrow hole, then pulled each tiny black button — twelve of them — through the leather flap. When fastened, they made a neat row from her instep to above her ankle. She felt like a real lady. There was plenty of space in the toes, enough to last a long time as she grew into them. She would save her old pair for Minnie.

Last, Nessa put on her mother's yellow hat. It was a proper outfit for a proper schoolteacher. She caught her reflection in the mirror and felt proud to also be wearing

Mrs. Lockett's blue dress, the prettiest regular dress she had ever owned.

As Nessa closed her trunk, she glanced out the window. Something at the creek made her heart jolt. An encampment of tepees. Smoke from a cooking fire rose into the trees. Nessa noticed a woman with long black hair carrying a child on her hip into the water. Beyond the campsite, dozens of horses grazed in the golden grass.

It seemed there were several families. Nessa wondered if they would camp there all winter. Or perhaps they were near the fort to do some trading.

She glanced out the window again before going downstairs. Mrs. Lockett was looking out the open back door, at the Indians.

"Honey, here's your dinner pail," she said. "I'm just glad you and the children'll be inside the fort today."

The library at Fort Larned was small compared to the schoolhouse. There was one tall bookshelf, arranged neatly from top to bottom, with an assortment of army manuals, songbooks, and novels. The walls were whitewashed, and in the corner was a tiny iron stove that stood just one foot tall. Its black stem poked through a hole in the low ceiling. Lieutenant Sullivan had made a fire early that morning so the room was warm enough for the girls to hang up their shawls. The dirt floor was freshly swept.

A square table with benches on each side occupied the space. On one wall was a round oak clock and next to it a photograph of President Abraham Lincoln, a black banner draped over its frame. Seven months had passed since his assassination. There was not yet a portrait of the country's new president, Andrew Johnson, so no one here knew what that man looked like.

A window gave a view of the parade ground where soldiers were marching in formation. The *rat-a-tat-tat* of drums filled the cool autumn air.

"Good morning, boys and girls," said Nessa, trying to draw their attention away from the window. "I'm thankful to God that we're all together again, and I'm grateful the post commander is letting us hold class here until our school is rebuilt, maybe by next week." Nessa smiled at her students because she was happy to see them, but also because she felt so good in her new shoes. They were warm, and the leather was soft. As Nessa stood in front of her students, she even felt a little taller.

"Well," she continued, "since the fire burned my Bible, I brought something else to read to you. It belonged to my mother."

Nessa held up a tiny leather book, just two-and-one-half inches square. Stamped on the front in tiny gold lettering was BELIEVER'S DAILY TREASURE. It was organized by the month, with a scripture for every day of the year.

Last night when she was looking through her trunk, she discovered this devotional tucked among her mother's drawings. It was so small she hadn't noticed it before. Her mother's name, Claire Christine, was written inside with the date 1852, and the binding had been mended with blue thread.

Carefully, Nessa turned the worn pages.

"Today's scripture is a pleasant coincidence," she said.

"But Mrs. Lockett told me that with God, there's no such thing as a coincidence. Anyway, it's called 'Of Deliverance from Danger,' from Lamentations three, verses fifty-seven and fifty-eight: *'Thou drewest near in the day that I called upon thee: thou saidst, Fear not.*

"'*O Lord, thou hast pleaded the causes of my soul; thou hast redeemed my life.'*

"Children, this verse reminds me of when we were under the blanket. I was so scared and worried I couldn't think of the right words to say, but you all prayed, anyway. I'm proud of you. We're here today because God answered your prayers. He delivered us from danger."

The room was quiet except for the clicking of the clock's second hand. It was nine-thirty. From outside came the sound of a bugler playing a marching tune, accompanied by the roll of drums. Nessa liked the rhythm of the soldiers' steps and how sharp they looked in their blue coats. Their golden epaulets matched their belt buckles and buttons. Next her eyes fell on the path beside the parade ground where a Negro girl was walking toward the library, a basket over her arm.

The girl knocked on the door, but would not come inside when Nessa invited her. She handed the basket to the teacher.

"These here're for you, from Cap'n Webster's wife," she said. "Her boys ain't in school, but she want to pay her respects, anyhow."

Nessa looked under the cloth. The aroma of warm biscuits stuffed with ham made her feel hungry.

"Oh, thank you." She looked at the girl's dark face and

guessed she was about twelve years old. Her black hair was braided into several short pigtails. "What's your name?" Nessa asked.

The servant backed away, dipping her head with shyness.

"I be Clementine, miss."

"Well, Clementine, please tell Mrs. Webster thank you from all of us. This is so kind of her."

At that moment, Nessa thought she would burst with happiness. Captain Webster's wife was one of the ladies she'd seen at the seamstress shop after Peter's death. She could not forget how the woman had made cruel remarks and said she would never trust Nessa with her little boy. But now this. A gift.

Clementine left with a curtsy. Watching her walk down the path, Nessa wanted to invite her to school but wondered if her mistress would allow it. After a moment, she turned back to her students.

"What a nice surprise," she said. "Let's eat these biscuits while they're still warm and —"

Another knock came at the door. Hoss walked in, his hair standing up straight like a stiff brush. "Pardon me, Miss Vanessa," he said. "Me and the sail maker went in together and bought these for your students. And here's paper from my cousin." He set a small stack of brown newsprint on the table with seven pencils and seven sticks of peppermint, striped blue and red.

Before Nessa could thank him he said, "Here's what. On account of the treaties, Indians are here today at Fort Larned to collect their annuities. That's a fancy word for food and weapons. Treaties mean we're all tryin' to get along. So don't be afraid, children."

Sven raised his hand. "Sir?" he asked in his husky voice. "Is the army giving guns and bullets to them?"

"That's right. Along with blankets, victuals, and such. Well, I'll be seein' you young'uns later. Learn your ABCs good, now."

Nessa looked out the window at the soldiers. Her cheerfulness suddenly faded. There was no reason she should fear Indians, other than from what she'd read in newspapers and heard from travelers. But now she remembered the attack on Fort Dodge last June. A small band of warriors stole horses then killed two sutlers, men who had been close friends of Ivy's father. And recently, another band burned down a rancher's barn before stealing all his stock.

She wasn't going to tell this to her students, however. They looked up at her from their seats, their faces a mixture of curiosity and concern. She realized that Hoss's comments had not reassured them.

"Children," she finally said, "a few weeks ago I came face-to-face with an Indian boy about my age when I was out at the cemetery visiting Peter's grave. I don't know what tribe he was from, but he had nice eyes and a beautiful horse. He rode away before I could ask his name. He didn't try to hurt me. So, as Hoss said, you shouldn't be afraid."

CHAPTER THIRTY-FIVE

———◆———

All in One Day

The next day was Saturday. When the fort's bugler played reveille, Nessa and Mrs. Lockett had already been in the kitchen for an hour. It was still dark out, but they were preparing chickens for the noon meal.

"'Morning," they said to Rolly when he came downstairs. He picked up the milking pail and headed for the back door, so sleepy he merely lifted his hand in greeting.

Today the schoolhouse was to be rebuilt, and there would be many hungry mouths to feed.

Mrs. Lockett's kitchen had a sour smell from the scalded chicken feathers. Mrs. Lockett had butchered the hens earlier and now was dipping them in boiling water. The feathers plucked out easily and later would be washed and dried to fill pillows.

"By the time the sun's overhead, those men will be hungry as wolves," she said. "And before we know it, Prairie River'll have a new schoolhouse, Nessa, and a fine Sunday church."

When Minnie woke up, she helped Nessa make pies.

They filled the pans with layers of canned peaches, almonds, cinnamon, and honey, then covered them with the dough Nessa had rolled out. She showed Minnie how to poke a hole so steam could escape, then sprinkle white sugar on top. While the pies were baking, Mrs. Lockett called them to breakfast. The delicious aroma of spices took over the room until they could no longer smell feathers.

Mrs. Lockett served them bread with crisp bacon, then poured them hot tea. It was one of Nessa's favorite breakfasts, and she loved it when it was just the four of them in this warm kitchen. Sitting across from Rolly and next to Minnie, she periodically felt them kick each other in the playful manner of siblings teasing each other. This morning, it was Nessa's turn to be kicked under the table. When she looked up, Rolly was grinning at her.

She felt like a real sister.

They loaded Rolly's cart with the roast chickens, biscuits, butter, pies, and a small tub of pickles from the cellar.

When they arrived at the school site, men had already been busy for hours. The walls that hadn't burned were being strengthened by more strips of sod at their base.

Nessa saw Mr. Applewood and Hoss lifting a wooden beam to hold up the roof. This was the ridgepole. Mr. Filmore and a young private helped them balance it into place. She marveled at how many people were laboring together, most of whom she'd never met. Timber for the support beams had been cut during the past few days from trees along the river.

Lieutenant Sullivan was there, wearing dungarees and a dark blue shirt. Only his wide-brimmed hat with gold braiding revealed he was an officer. He and another soldier were driving the mules with Mr. Button's grasshopper plow to cut sod in an area unmarked by the fire. The plow was so named because its high, rounded shape resembled a grasshopper's legs. Some men were cutting sod bricks one foot wide and two feet long, cutting deep into the soil where the grassy roots tangled tightly together. Others followed behind and carefully lifted the strips, then carried them to the schoolhouse. These they laid on top of the last level, grass side down, two bricks wide, to form a wall two feet thick.

Nearby, Mrs. Lockett and some of the students' mothers were unloading picnic baskets and setting up tables. When Nessa noticed Fanny Jo also helping, she felt a nervous flutter in her stomach, but was distracted by someone calling her name.

"Want another window, Miss Vanessa?" a man asked when he had gotten her attention. "We can make space for a new one, then build the walls around it, easy." He was pushing a cart filled with slabs of lumber to frame the windows. The sills would also be as wide as the walls, roomy enough for a child to sit with a book.

She walked through the doorway and looked into the open room. Overhead, white clouds streaked across the sky, casting thin shadows on the dirt floor. "Another window would be wonderful," she told him. "The light makes it easier to read on dark days. Thank you, sir."

"Anything you say, miss." He tipped his hat and smiled at her. Nessa was delighted to be asked her opinion. How good it felt to be regarded as the permanent teacher.

Nessa then turned her gaze to Fanny Jo, who was arranging spoons and dinner plates on a table. Her dress hung loosely around her middle and the fringe on her shawl dangled in the wind. Nessa hadn't seen her since that terrible, hot day and felt nervous about approaching her. In her mind Nessa counted *one . . . two . . . three* to build her courage, then walked over to the table.

"Fanny Jo . . . hello," she said. "How are you?"

Fanny Jo turned toward Nessa. Her cheeks were rosy and her swept-up hair had wisps blowing around her face. "Nessa," she said softly, "I don't know what to say to you."

Nessa lowered her eyes to the ground.

"It's going to take a while," Fanny Jo continued, "for things to be sorted out. Not that you need to know any of this, but I'll tell you anyway — someone in town wrote our father with dirty rumors, and he has since contacted the commander here at Fort Larned with orders for us to return East." She brushed a lock of hair from her eyes as she regarded Nessa. "This brings more complications because my husband is still assigned to Fort Dodge, and I do not intend to leave without first seeing him and being safely delivered of our child. Most dreadful of all, he received word that *I* was divorcing *him*."

Now Nessa felt worse than ever. Her one little tale told to Ivy had spread far and wide into an ugly mess. As she looked at the blackened grass around them, she realized her mistake was no different than a prairie fire that had begun with just one tiny spark.

At this, Laura arrived with an armful of sage for the table. She stuffed the stems into a jar of water. She glanced up at her sister, but said nothing. After a moment of awkward silence, Nessa twisted her hands in her apron.

"I'm so sorry," she said. "I hope someday you'll be able to forgive me. . . . I . . . oh, Fanny Jo and Laura, you have every right to be mad at me, but I hate it that you are and that there's nothing I can do —"

Nessa grabbed the hem of her skirt and hurried away from the picnic area, swallowing hard to keep from crying. She so wanted to be friends with the sisters. How she wished Ivy was well enough to stand at her side.

Nessa tried to hide her distress. She busied herself by keeping an eye on the children, to make sure none of them wandered off alone.

It made her feel good to see so much activity and people working together. Rolly and Sven were carrying sod bricks for the walls, and the girls were helping their mothers set out the noon meal. Poppy was standing under Wildwing's neck, reaching up to pet him. There were smaller children too young for school, chasing one another in circles with the help of Green.

Nessa found Mrs. Lockett looking off toward the creek. Swaths of blackened brush blended into the tall grass not touched by fire. The garden looked like a bare island.

"Mrs. Lockett? Are you all right?"

The wind was blowing the woman's apron strings behind her like the tails of a kite. She adjusted her shawl around her shoulders and turned to Nessa. Her cheeks were damp.

"Honey," she said, "I'm just grateful, that's all."

CHAPTER THIRTY-SIX

A Debt Paid

By sunset, the last plank of wood was laid over the roof beams and glass panes were set into the windows. Mr. Bell, the blacksmith, carried in a new door with strong iron hinges and an iron latch. He and the tinsmith had repaired the stove and made a new chimney pipe, extra long so it stretched across the room just beneath the ceiling. Wires from the overhead rafters held it in place. This extra length would give off more heat and was up high enough so the children wouldn't bump their heads.

Shingles for the roof were made from tin cans that Hoss and Mr. Button had hammered flat. But there had only been enough for one slope.

"We'll keep collecting empty cans in town," Hoss announced to everyone. His stiff hair ruffled in the wind. "Then our school will have a roof no fire can touch. Oh, and we're ready for church tomorrow, ten o'clock. Bring something to sit on and a picnic to share afterward."

At the end of the service the next day, Hoss came up front with his guitar. In his deep, smooth voice he began singing.

> *"Amazing grace! How sweet the sound —*
> *That saved a wretch like me!*
> *I once was lost but now am found,*
> *Was blind but now I see.*
>
> *"'Twas grace that taught my heart to fear,*
> *And grace my fears relieved;*
> *How precious did that grace appear*
> *The hour I first believed!*
>
> *"Through many dangers, toils, and snares,*
> *I have already come;*
> *'Tis grace hath brought me safe thus far,*
> *And grace will lead me home. . . ."*

Nessa sang these words from her heart. Though Hoss was only nineteen, he seemed much older to her. She liked how his rough hands strummed the delicate strings and how he closed his eyes to savor the music. The words brought tears as she reflected on them. *Through many dangers, toils, and snares . . . 'tis grace hath brought me safe thus far . . . Thank You again, Lord — for the hundredth time, thank You — for leading me to Prairie River and for bringing us safely out of the fire.*

Nearly fifty people were crowded inside the school-house on assorted benches, chairs, and stools. There were now five windows, two on each opposite wall and one high up by the rafters. The sunlight coming in over its wide sill cast light across the beams, giving the room a cheerful atmosphere.

Though it was sunny, a cold wind rattled the panes. Nessa could see miles of prairie grass rippling like water, and flocks of soaring birds. She wished Albert were sitting beside her to see it all, to meet her new friends. During the closing prayer, she again asked God to look after her old friend.

Nessa walked with Green to the Applewoods' store. Her shoes gave her a new confidence, for she felt more respectable. Wearing something that wasn't scuffed or patched or previously thrown out by someone else made her feel special.

The bell against the door jingled when she opened it. No one was at the counter so Nessa waited, admiring a bolt of blue cloth. Just as her fingers touched the soft cotton, Mrs. Applewood stepped into the room.

Nessa snatched her hand back, afraid she would be reprimanded, but the rebuke never came.

"Yes?" asked the woman.

Taking the mangled deck of cards from her apron pocket, Nessa held them up.

"Mrs. Applewood" — she spoke rapidly to avoid being called a thief — "I need to pay you for these because the last time I was here Green took them while I wasn't looking, and I didn't notice until I got home — I'm really sorry — then the next day was the fire, and I've been meaning to come tell you and pay for them, but at this moment this is all I have. . . ."

She put her ten pennies on the counter. "I'll pay you the rest as soon as possible, when —"

Mrs. Applewood held up her hand for Nessa to stop talking. "You mean to tell me this yellow dog here stole a deck of playing cards?"

"Yes, ma'am." Green sat at Nessa's feet, wagging her tail and looking up at Mrs. Applewood.

The woman turned away. The back of her neck stiffened and her shoulders began to shake. Nessa at first thought she was crying, but such a laugh escaped from Mrs. Applewood that Nessa felt herself laugh, too. Still, she was unsure what to do, knowing her history with the woman.

At last, Mrs. Applewood turned around. She scooped the pennies into her palm and looked at Nessa. Her tight lips moved upward into the faintest smile. It appeared to Nessa as if her eyes were moist.

"Consider it even, child," she said. "And tell your dog she can keep the cards."

CHAPTER THIRTY-SEVEN

Invitation

The next day, Nessa woke with a new confidence. In a raw wind, she walked to Officers' Row, to Captain Webster's quarters. When Clementine opened the door, a savory aroma of fried meat and onions came from the tiny kitchen.

"How are you, Clementine?" Nessa asked.

"I be good, miss."

"May I speak to Mrs. Webster, please?"

"Yes, miss, come in."

There was a swish of a satin dress as the captain's wife entered the room. Her hoopskirt squeezed between a red velvet sofa and chair as she came forward to greet Nessa.

"Hello, dear. You must be here about my boys coming to school."

Nessa paused and her gaze moved to Clementine. "Yes, ma'am," she said, looking back at the officer's wife. Another reason for Nessa's visit had to do with the servant girl standing before them, but she wasn't sure how to say so. "How old are your sons?" she asked.

"Seven and eight," said the woman. "They're good boys."

At that moment, a ruckus broke out in the back room. There was the sound of a heavy piece of furniture being dragged across the floor, a thump, and small voices arguing. A crash of breaking glass startled Nessa so that she turned to look in its direction.

"Don't worry," the woman said. "Matilda's tending to them." Nessa nodded, assuming Matilda must be Clementine's mother.

Nessa felt awkward. She hadn't been invited to sit or to come warm herself, so she continued standing, her hands behind her back. The room had a square piano and another red chair by the window. A small iron stove in the corner gave off heat. A kitten playing behind a drape started swinging by its claws, ripping the lace as it descended to the floor. Nessa swallowed hard to keep from laughing. This amusing sight gave her courage.

"Mrs. Webster, I came to also invite Clementine to school. She's most welcome, and I'd love to have her for a student, along with your sons."

The woman's smile faded. Her hands were folded at her corseted waist. "Oh," she said, "I'm afraid that's not possible, my boys sitting in the same classroom as Clementine."

Nessa waited. When no explanation came, she said, "May I inquire as to why, ma'am?"

An angry look clouded the woman's face. "Now, you see here, young lady. You've no right to question me. Evidently you've forgotten your place by daring to come here. This area is for officers of the United States Army and their families. Why, you don't even *have* a family."

Mrs. Webster motioned for Clementine to open the

door. "Good day and good-bye," the woman said to Nessa.

On her way out, Nessa glanced back at Clementine and noticed the girl had a hopeful look in her eyes.

As she headed home into the wind, her shawl over her head for warmth, Nessa walked along the sidewalk reserved for the family members of officers. The sound of her new shoes on the planks lifted her spirits. She even kicked her foot a bit to see her petticoat.

For one brief moment the woman's words — *you don't even have a family* — had cut at Nessa's heart. But then she pictured Mrs. Lockett in the kitchen, with Rolly and Minnie at the table teasing each other. She pictured reading to Ivy and how her father called both of them "sweetheart." There was Poppy, the way she leaned into Nessa's skirt when they would stand together looking out at the prairie. Then she thought about the big cousins, Mr. Button and Hoss, who always had treats for Green and Wildwing.

Nessa smiled as her shoes clicked along the sidewalk. No family? Mrs. Webster didn't know what she was talking about.

CHAPTER THIRTY-EIGHT

Abraham Lincoln Said

Hoss walked into the kitchen holding a dead bird by its feet. It was larger than a duck and had bare skin on its head and neck. Nessa thought it resembled three feather dusters tied together.

"Turkey, Miss Vivian," he told her. "For tomorrow's dinner."

Mrs. Lockett took the bird and set it on the table. "Hoss, you're a good fellow, thank you kindly. You're comin', ain't you? And Mr. Button, too, I hope?"

"Oh, yes, ma'am. Wouldn't miss it." He smiled shyly at Nessa.

Nessa felt herself flush. She turned away and started filling the large kettle with water that had been heating on the stove. They would need to scald the turkey so its feathers could easily be pulled out. "What's tomorrow?" she asked.

"Why, it's Thanksgiving, dear," said Mrs. Lockett. She set a bowl of brown sugar on the table with a small pitcher of cream, then poured Hoss a cup of coffee. She gestured to the bench, inviting him to seat himself.

"Official holiday, Nessa," he told her. He held the cup in his calloused hands and took a noisy slurp. After swallowing, he gazed up at the ceiling in thought. "Let's see — this is what Button told me — two years ago, in sixty-three, President Lincoln decided the fourth Thursday of every November should be special. A day for us Americans to gather together and give thanks. Here's what, this afternoon we'll bring you a smoked ham from the sutlers, so there'll be more than plenty to go around. We weren't sure how many boarders you have, but we want to do our part. Anything else I can get for you?"

"My word, no," she said. "You've done more than enough."

"Well, thank you much," he said. He took another slurp. Cream coated his upper lip. "There's no doubt, Miss Vivian, you make the best coffee in Prairie River — strong and hot, just how I like it."

Before the holiday supper, everyone helped with the last-minute preparations. Boards were placed on top of stools to make two extra tables in the parlor, in front of the fireplace. Hoss moved the sofa and wingback chairs onto the front porch to make room, then helped Minnie shake out the tablecloths and spread them nicely to cover the rough wood. The cloths were festive, red-and-white checks. Mr. Button made centerpieces from handfuls of acorns arranged on a doily.

Rolly drove his cart to town. He and Mr. Filmore wrapped Ivy in Nessa's buffalo robe with stones that had been heated in the oven. This meant she would be warm riding in back out of the wind. When they arrived at the boardinghouse, Nessa positioned her friend in the warmest corner of the kitchen and gave her a footstool to keep her feet off the cold floor.

Soon, Laura arrived with Fanny Jo, who looked quite expectant under her full cloak. Their cheeks were red from their walk in the cold, and they carried a basket with three small pies and a pot of beans that had been baked in honey. To Nessa's delight, the sisters smiled at her and reached out to touch her hand as they came in the front door.

Laura leaned close. "Nessa," she whispered, "we used the pumpkins from your school garden for these pies. I just know they're going to be delicious."

Moments later, Mr. and Mrs. Bell drove up the creek road in their wagon. Baby Oliver was so bundled, he looked like a sack of flour when they brought him inside. The blacksmith's wife made a special point of telling Nessa that their jug of pickled cucumbers had also come from the harvest of her garden.

Mrs. Lockett flurried about the kitchen as Minnie and Nessa helped her set out platters of roast turkey and ham. There were bowls of gravy, mashed turnips and potatoes, corn, beets, green beans, and fresh applesauce. Loaves of dark rye bread were in the center of each table, with plates of fresh butter.

Mr. Filmore stood by the stove to give the blessing. He wore his patchwork vest and a new string tie. "Folks," he said, "it's our first Thanksgiving since the war ended, and I know we're all mighty thankful for that."

He bowed his head. *"Lord Jesus, we pray You will bless our country with many more years of peace and help us be friends with our neighbors here. We thank You for Mrs. Lockett's hard work today and ask You to bless her and every person in this house, and please protect these travelers when they continue their journey. Thank You, dear Lord, for all You've provided and may this food nourish us. . . . Amen."*

Counting the travelers who were boarding with Mrs. Lockett, there were eighteen at dinner. Nessa sat between two brothers from New York who were on their way to California. Across from her was a shoemaker who had come to Fort Larned to work for the army. He was clean-shaven and his hair was pulled back into a ponytail. When she asked his name, he laughed so hard, food fell out of his mouth.

"Here's something funny, miss," he said. "For six generations back my family's been makin' boots and shoes for old and young, rich and poor, fat, skinny, tall and short, every kind you can imagine. But I'll bet you can't guess my name."

Nessa liked his cheerful manner and the way his eyes lit up when he talked. She thought a moment, then shrugged. "What is it?" she asked.

The man laughed again. He leaned over a platter of turkey to shake her hand. "Fancy Shoemaker, at your service," he said. "Honest to God, that's my name. 'Fancy' after an uncle who was a preacher, and 'Shoemaker' after all my grandpas before me." He was so enthusiastic, he stood up to shake hands with everyone else at the table, then worked his way into the kitchen, his napkin still tucked into his collar. His high-heel boots were freshly polished.

As Nessa watched Fancy Shoemaker introduce himself to Hoss and the others, she found herself smiling with happiness. She liked the guests who stayed in the boardinghouse, and she liked this new holiday. She hadn't really known about Thanksgiving because there'd been no special dinner at the orphanage. Thanks to Mrs. Lockett, Nessa was beginning to forget what it was like to feel hungry all the time.

It was a wonderful day. And best of all, Fanny Jo and Laura were no longer angry with her.

After dinner, Mr. Button stood up and unfolded a newspaper clipping from his vest pocket. His large stomach provided a shelf upon which to set his spectacles. Putting them on so he could see the small print, he said, "This here is something our good President Lincoln said before he died. Because this day of Thanksgiving was his idea, I want to honor him by sharing his thoughts with you folks.

"I leave you, hoping that the lamp of liberty will burn in your bosoms until there shall no longer be a doubt that all men are created free and equal."

"Here, here," came the chorus of voices.

Nessa looked around the room at the travelers and her friends. She and Ivy exchanged smiles. While helping Mrs. Lockett dish up plates of pie, Nessa reflected on this day of thanksgiving. More than ever, she appreciated her new life in Prairie River. And she loved Mr. Lincoln's words. They made her feel hopeful for the peace treaties with the Indians and especially for Clementine. Maybe over time Nessa could convince Mrs. Webster to let the girl come to school after all.

CHAPTER THIRTY-NINE

One Gray Afternoon

After lunch the next day, Rolly ran up the porch, waving a letter in his hand. "Mother!" he cried. "For you. From Washington . . . And Nessa, you got one, too."

Mrs. Lockett lowered herself into a chair by the stove as Rolly burst through the kitchen door. Cold air swept in with bits of leaves and dried grass. When he gave her the letter, her hands started shaking.

"What's it say, Mama?" asked Minnie.

They all stared at the envelope. Someone with elegant penmanship had addressed it to Mrs. Charles Lockett, Prairie River, Kansas. In the upper left corner were a stranger's initials.

W. W.

ARMORY SQUARE HOSPITAL

WASHINGTON CITY

"Oh, dear," she said. "Who's this from?"

Nessa put the kettle on for tea and set out cups and saucers. This comforting gesture was one she had learned from Mrs. Lockett. She glanced at her letter that Rolly had placed on the table and recognized Albert's handwriting. She slipped it into her apron pocket to read alone upstairs.

The room was quiet except for the wind rattling the kitchen window. A draft was seeping in from under the door, making the floor cold. The woman turned the letter over and held it up to the light to see if she could read through the thin paper.

"I'm just afraid of what it might say," she whispered.

The boiling water on the stove began to splash. Using a ladle, Nessa filled the china teapot, then added mint leaves and a stick of cinnamon. As the tea steeped, Rolly and Minnie stood up and moved over to the table, regarding their mother with concern.

"Do you think it's about Pa?" asked Rolly, taking a seat.

She nodded. "I fear so, children." The family sat in silence.

Nessa set out a plate of shortbread, then poured their tea. Mrs. Lockett breathed in the steamy aroma from her cup and closed her eyes.

"Thank you, darlin'," she said.

It was a gray afternoon. Two gentlemen were in the parlor reading by firelight, and a lady guest was upstairs napping. Outside, storm clouds darkened the sky. The air had smelled of snow when Rolly came in with the letters.

Mrs. Lockett's cup clattered against its saucer as she set it down. She took a deep breath. "Nessa, honey, would you mind readin' the letter to us?"

Nessa took the envelope and sat on the bench beside

Minnie. With her thumbnail, she cracked the wax seal and slid out a folded piece of stationery. Her heart was in her throat. What if it was terrible news? How would she keep her voice calm? She wouldn't be able to bear seeing this family heartbroken.

"Dear Madam,

I write on behalf of your husband, Captain Charles Solomon Lockett. This moment I am at his bedside in Ward A while he sleeps —"

Nessa looked up, hopeful.
"Continue, dear," said Mrs. Lockett.

"— recovering from pneumonia and surgery. He has asked me to send this correspondence to let you know he will come home as soon as he is well enough to make the journey —"

A gasp came from Mrs. Lockett. "Oh, my good Lord," she said, her eyes filling with tears. "Keep going, Nessa."

"— He sends his deepest affection to you, madam, and to his son and daughter. Be assured, he rests comfortably on a cot and shall be transferred to a bed as soon as one is available. He requested I read to him from the Scriptures, which I do upon each visit, and he enjoys the figs and sweet crackers brought by a kindhearted citizen named Mrs. Henley.

"Over the past months, I have made the acquaintances of soldiers and officers in Washington's hospital wards and have had the pleasure of conversing with, and writing letters for, many an honorable man, loyal to his country and devoted to his family. Your husband, madam, is one of them.

"I remain, yours truly, Walt Whitman — 10 August 1865"

Nessa looked up to see Rolly and Minnie embracing their mother, who was weeping in their arms.

It was the most joyful news Nessa had heard since the war ended. She felt as happy as if this were her own dear father.

No one asked the question why Mr. Lockett was unable to write his own letter or noticed that it had taken more than three months to reach Prairie River.

Only one thing mattered. Captain Lockett had survived the war, and he was returning to his family.

Before supper, Nessa found Rolly in front of the fireplace, reading.

"What's that?" she asked, sitting on the hearth beside him.

"Mr. Whitman's letter," he said. "He must be a good man to do such a kindness, don't you think, Nessa?"

She looked at Rolly's blue eyes and the moisture gathering there. She felt tenderness for him, as if they were truly brother and sister. "Yes, I think so, Rolly."

CHAPTER FORTY

———◆———

Where the Wind Always Blows

Green loped ahead of Nessa as she walked to the cemetery, carrying a pail to water Peter's tiny oak tree. Her hands were numb when she set the bucket on the hard ground. As she faced the wind, her unbraided hair blew behind her. The long sleeves of her red dress and its length kept her warmer than her old clothes, but by winter she would need a wool cloak to keep out the cold. She tightened her shawl around her shoulders and throat.

It is lonesome yet beautiful out here, she thought, looking toward the trail. Two rabbits bounded out of their hiding place, zigzagging in front of Green as she gave chase. At their approach, clusters of birds flew up from the grass, chittering in complaint.

Nessa sat in a small hollow of earth, out of the wind, and lay back to look at the sky. Albert's letter was in her sleeve. Already she had read it twice, but wanted it close to her while she considered what he had said.

His first piece of news had thrilled her, but the information he shared next had made her blood run cold. Nessa could hardly believe it when she read he was saving money to come to Prairie River. Even if the position were taken at Mr. Button's newspaper, he said he would find work just so they could be together once more.

She read the next part of the letter again, holding it tight so the wind wouldn't snatch it from her fingers. Green lay next to her, head on paws, watching Nessa's face.

> . . . when I saw the Reverend he was stomping mad about his letter coming back to him. He knows you're in Prairie River because the ticket man described you and how you got on the stage back in April. Soon as McDuff can settle his affairs here, he says he's coming to claim what the Lord said is his. Nessa, I will be there soonly. DO NOT MARRY HIM.
> Your friend from days long past,
> Albert

Nessa closed her eyes. It was soothing listening to the cries of geese overhead and wind moving through the grass. There was nothing she could do at this moment to keep Reverend McDuff from getting on a stagecoach headed for Kansas. She had prayed and cried and pleaded with God, but still the man was coming.

In the meantime, Nessa was comforted knowing Mrs. Lockett would not let him stay at the boardinghouse. Also, she was the schoolteacher with a job she loved to do, and she had friends. She had her own horse and a dog that followed her everywhere.

As the wind blew her hair off her neck, Nessa drew her knees up inside her dress for warmth. Doing so, she admired the fine black stitches along her sleeves, sewn so carefully by Mrs. Lockett. With her fingers, she traced the black piping of her hem, then lifted it slightly to peek at her shoes. The smooth leather of Ivy's gift was still a marvel to her. Just for fun, she tapped her toes together. *Clothed in friendship,* she thought.

Nessa no longer felt alone.

And, she smiled, Albert was coming.

About the Author

Kristiana Gregory was born in Los Angeles, California. She has always wanted to be a writer and received her first rejection letter (for a poem) at age eleven. After graduating from high school, she began taking a variety of college courses and jobs, including positions as a daily news reporter for the *San Luis Obispo Telegram-Tribune*, and a book reviewer for the *Los Angeles Times*, that helped prepare her for her writing career. Her first book, *Jenny of the Tetons*, won the Golden Kite Award for fiction. She has contributed numerous titles to Scholastic's Dear America and Royal Diaries series. Kristiana has also written several books about the Old West and California history. *Earthquake at Dawn*, her book about the 1906 San Francisco earthquake, won the 1993 California Book Award for best juvenile fiction.

Married for twenty-one years, she lives in Boise, Idaho, with her husband and two golden retrievers. Their two sons, college students, live nearby and often drop by around dinnertime.

What will happen to Nessa when Reverend McDuff comes to town?

PRAIRIE RIVER

A WINTER SONG

KRISTIANA GREGORY

It is December of 1865, and Nessa feels safe and at home in Prairie River. But when Reverend McDuff arrives unexpectedly at the Lockett's boardinghouse, Nessa's hopes of leaving her past behind are shattered. Only Ivy and Mrs. Lockett know her secret — her reason for fleeing Independence and heading west. Now she's afraid the town will judge her unfairly and her position as a schoolteacher could be lost forever. In what promises to be a long and fierce winter in Prairie River, Nessa must be stronger than ever.

www.scholastic.com/books

■SCHOLASTIC

MORE SERIES YOU'LL FALL IN LOVE WITH

TWITCHES

Imagine finding out you have an identical twin. Cam and Alex just did. Think nothing can top that? Guess again. (They also just learned they're witches.)

The AMAZING DAYS of ABBY HAYES

In a family of superstars, it's hard to stand out. But Abby is about to surprise her friends, her family, and most of all, herself!

Heartland™

Nestled in the foothills of Virginia, there's a place where horses come when they are hurt. Amy, Ty, and everyone at Heartland work together to heal the horses—and form lasting bonds that will touch your heart.

Learn more at
www.scholastic.com/books

Available Wherever Books Are Sold.

Every family has something to hide.

Ever wonder if your family has secrets you don't know? Hattie Owen didn't.

At least not until the startling arrival of an uncle whom she never knew she had. He turns her world upside down, and she's forced to look beyond the comfortable routine of her small-town life.

Newbery Honor Book

When everything falls apart, the best thing to do is to stick together.

Belle Teal's life isn't easy, but she gets by. She lives with her mother and grandmother far out in the country. They don't have much money, but she feels rich with their love. However, as a new school year begins, Belle Teal faces unexpected challenges and big problems.

www.scholastic.com